# MURDER, SHE WROTE:
# MURDER AT THE
# POWDERHORN RANCH

# MURDER, SHE WROTE: MURDER AT THE POWDERHORN RANCH

Jessica Fletcher & Donald Bain

Chivers Press • G.K. Hall & Co.
Bath, England Thorndike, Maine USA

This Large Print edition is published by Chivers Press, England, and by G.K. Hall & Co., USA.

Published in 2000 in the U.K. by arrangement with Universal.

Published in 2000 in the U.S. by arrangement with Chivers Press, Ltd.

U.K. Hardcover   ISBN 0-7540-4019-4   (Chivers Large Print)
U.K. Softcover   ISBN 0-7540-4020-8   (Camden Large Print)
U.S. Softcover   ISBN 0-7838-8926-7   (Nightingale Series Edition)

The text of this Large Print edition is unabridged.
Other aspects of the book may vary from the original edition.

Set in 16 pt. New Times Roman.

Printed in Great Britain on acid-free paper.

**British Library Cataloguing in Publication Data available**

**Library of Congress Cataloging-in-Publication Data**

Bain, Donald, 1935–
    Murder at the Powderhorn Ranch : a Murder, she wrote
    mystery : a novel / by Jessica Fletcher and Donald Bain.
        p.    cm.
    "Based on the Universal television series created by Peter S.
Fischer, Richard Levinson & William Link."
    ISBN 0-7838-8926-7 (lg. print : sc : alk. paper)
    1. Fletcher, Jessica (Fictitious character)—Fiction.
    2. Women detectives—Fiction.    3. Women novelists—Fiction.
    4. Large type books.    I. Title.
    PS3552.A376 M3      2000
    813'.54—dc21                                      99–056673

For Danielle Perez and Cindy Chang

For the *real* cowboys and cowgirls: Joseph
Webber, Mandy Nesbitt, Joel and Melanie
Fonder, Amber Kilgore, Jon Sadler, Andy
Wallace, and Tobi Whitaker

And with special thanks to
the Colorado Dude and Guest Ranch
Association

# CHAPTER ONE

'Nice and easy, Jessica. Don't jerk the controls. just a little nudge here, a slight turn there, and the plane pretty much flies itself.'

I gently, tentatively placed my hands on the control yoke of the single-engine Cessna 172 and moved it an inch to the left. The plane responded by starting a slow turn.

'That's it, Jessica,' Jed said in his low, calm voice. 'See how easy it is?'

Jed Richardson had been a top commercial airline pilot for years before moving to Cabot Cove to start his own small charter airline, flying out of a bare-bones, compact airport on the town's southern edge. Jed is a central-casting image of a pilot, a wry, knowing, infectious grin always on his round, tanned, deeply creased face. He wore his usual uniform, a distressed brown leather aviator's jacket, white silk scarf about his neck, and a blue peaked cap with Jed's Flying Service emblazoned in gold on it.

'This is so exciting,' I said, barely able to control my glee.

'Makes you feel free, doesn't it?' he said, smiling. 'As many years as I've been doing it, I always get a little excited when I take off. Look down, Jess. Pretty sight, huh?'

Below and to my right was Cabot Cove, laid out neatly before me.

1

'Let's go take a look at your house. Turn right. While you do, add a little rudder pedal with your right foot. Makes for a smoother turn. That's it, just a midge of pressure.'

A few minutes later, with Jed at the controls, we passed over my home.

'It looks so small from up here,' I said.

'Picture-perfect, isn't it?'

'Yes.'

I drew a deep breath, grinned, and peered through the windshield into the pristine, blue, late August sky that surrounded us. *You've done it*, I told myself. *You've actually done it!*

A half hour later, Jed had me guide the aircraft to the airport, make a series of turns that lined us up with the runway. 'We always land into the wind,' he said—then took the controls for a smooth touchdown. My first flying lesson was in the books, literally, as Jed filled out my spanking new flight log and signed off on the lesson.

'There's Doc Hazlitt,' Jed said, taxiing the Cessna to a corrugated metal hangar on which a large red Sign, JED'S FLYING SERVICE, glistened in the late morning sun. He shut down the engine, flipped some other switches, and reached across to open the door for me on the right side of the plane. I stepped down, patted the fuselage, and walked to where my good friend and Cabot Cove's leading physician, Seth Hazlitt, waited.

'Well, how was it?' he asked.

2

'Wonderful, Seth. A special feeling, so free, so liberating.'

Jed joined us. 'She'll make a fine pilot,' he said.

Seth grunted.

'Has a nice touch,' Jed continued. 'Real easy on the controls.'

'We flew over my house,' I said as we walked to where they'd parked their cars.

'Did you now?' Seth said.

Jed looked at me and winked. We both knew Seth was against my taking flying lessons. He offered myriad reasons: I didn't even drive a car; it wasn't ladylike; it was too dangerous; peering into the sun would give me lines around the eyes, as it had for Jed; and, I suspected, a modicum of jealousy.

\*　　\*　　\*

Seth had talked over the years of one day taking flying lessons, but never got around to it. When I suggested he sign up with me, he dismissed the notion as folly. 'Too old for such nonsense now,' he'd said.

'Too old? I never thought I'd hear you say that.'

'Takes a young person's reflexes,' he said.

'Not according to Jed. He says flying a plane is easier than driving a car.'

'Fine for him to say considerin' he's been doing it all his life. No, Jessica, I'll not be

3

taking flying lessons from Jed Richardson, or anybody else. And neither will you.'

I should explain the tenor of my relationship with Seth Hazlitt. We are the best of friends. I haven't the slightest doubt that he'd do almost anything for me, and has in the past. I, of course, would do the same. Because we are such good pals, we are quick to overlook our respective foibles and idiosyncrasies. Mine are legion, but Seth has his, too, the most evident of which is a tendency to try to keep close tabs on me, rein me in when he thinks I've reached too far, protect me and . . . well, on occasion, run my life. I know he means well, and I seldom allow him to nettle me. But he'd come close over the issue of my signing up with Jed Richardson for flying lessons.

\*　　\*　　\*

'Same time tomorrow?' Jed asked as we prepared to leave the airport.

'I'll be here,' I said.

Seth scowled.

'Lunch?' I asked Seth.

'Was plannin' on it.'

\*　　\*　　\*

After clam chowder and tuna fish sandwiches at Mara's Luncheonette on the town dock, Seth drove me home.

'Coffee?' I asked.

'Don't mind if I do.'

I admit to being somewhat of a coffee snob, and take pride in mixing flavors to come up with what I consider the perfect blend, at least to my taste. We settled at my kitchen table, breathed in the rich aroma from our mugs, touched rims, and sipped.

'Excellent, as usual,' he said.

'Thank you, for the compliment and for the lunch.'

'My pleasure. Jessica, about this flying lesson nonsense, I—'

'Pardon me for interrupting, Seth, but it isn't nonsense. It represents something I have the need to experience. Nothing nonsensical about that.'

'I suppose not. But I just can't figure out why you're doing it.'

I looked out the window to where birds fluttered about my ten-quart feeder, vying for space on the four perches. The sun cast a pretty pattern on my kitchen counter. I thought of the morning and my introduction to flying—not just being in a plane, even a small one; my frequent flier bank is overflowing— but to have placed my hands, and feet, on the controls and making the plane do what I wanted it to do. I broke into a grin.

'Pleasant thought you're havin', I take it.'

'Extremely pleasant.' I sat forward and placed my hands on one of his. 'Seth, haven't

5

you ever felt a compelling need to challenge yourself, to reach beyond what you're comfortable with and conquer something you'd always considered unattainable?'

' 'Course I have. Do it all the time.'

'I think we're talking about different things,' I said. 'I know you're always seeking new advances in medicine, and that you take courses to learn about subjects that interest you. You thoroughly enjoyed that series of cooking courses you took last year. And the seminar on collecting rare, first-edition books had you glowing. Remember?'

'*Ayuh*. Those were mind-expanding experiences.'

'They certainly were. But I've reached a point in my life where I feel a need to challenge myself physically. Run a marathon, climb a mountain, drive a race car—learn to fly.'

He said nothing.

'Don't you understand?'

'I suppose I do. I *think* I do. I just don't want you to be doing something that's dangerous.'

'I know, and I appreciate your concern. But flying a plane doesn't have to be dangerous. Jed says more people are killed every year at railroad crossings than die in airplane accidents around the world. He says—'

My defense of my newest hobby was interrupted by the ringing phone. I picked up.

'Jessica? Jim Cook.'

6

'Jim! What a pleasant surprise.'

Jim and Bonnie Cook had lived in Cabot Cove for years until fulfilling their dream of owning and operating a dude ranch out west. They looked at many ranches for sale in Colorado until deciding on an eighty-acre property in the town of Powderhorn, five hours southwest of Denver, nestled in the Powderhorn Valley and adjacent to more than a million acres of uninhabited wilderness. The closest commercial airport is a forty-five-minute drive from the ranch, in the town of Gunnison.

We threw a lavish going-away party for the Cooks when they left Cabot Cove. They were active, well-liked, respected members of the community. I'd kept in touch with them over the years via an occasional letter, phone call, and the yearly Christmas card. They'd invited me on many occasions to be their guest at the ranch. Unfortunately, my schedule never co-operated. The Powderhorn was open only from early June through mid-September.

After some preliminary chitchat, Jim said, 'Bonnie and I decided we won't take no for an answer this time.'

'About what?'

'About you coming out here to visit. We've got a horse all picked out for you, the trout are jumping, and one of our best cabins has your name on it. Besides, we're always looking for another square dance partner.'

Bonnie Cook got on an extension. 'Please come, Jess. It's been years. We miss you.'

'And I miss you, too.

'No excuses,' Jim said. 'If you're working on another book, we'll set you up with a computer.'

Seth indicated he wanted to join the conversation.

'I'm here with Seth Hazlitt,' I said. 'He wants to talk to you.' I handed him the phone.

'Howdy,' Seth said.

I refilled our coffee cups while he talked with the Cooks, half listening to what he was saying. But when I heard, 'Jessica and I would love to come out to the ranch,' he had my full attention.

'We?' I mouthed.

'Sounds good,' he said. 'That'll give us two weeks to get ourselves ready, clear my slate of patients for the week, and let Jessica get herself geared up to go.'

I retrieved the phone.

'Can't wait to see you,' Jim Cook said. 'It's a perfect week for you and Doc to come.'

'But I—'

'We'll send you all the info you'll need, travel arrangements, clothes to bring, stuff like that.'

'How wonderful we'll be seeing you again,' Bonnie Cook said. 'I can't wait for these next two weeks to pass.'

I looked at Seth, who sat at the table, hands

folded over his stomach, a satisfied smile on his face.

'Bonnie, Jim, can I get back to you?' I said. 'I have to . . . to handle something.'

'Of course,' said Jim. 'We'll be here all day. By the way, the week you'll be coming is perfect for us. The Morrison family picked that week for its annual reunion. They come every year. We don't book anybody else that week, which means we have three cabins available, one for you, one for the doc, and one empty one.'

'I wouldn't want to inconvenience this family,' I said.

'That's no problem, Jess. I asked them whether they'd mind having other guests, and they said they'd be honored to share the week with you. You're famous even out here in the wilds of Colorado.'

'I'll call you later, Jim.'

'We'll be waiting.'

'Well, Dr. Hazlitt,' I said after hanging up, 'I know you're my physician, but I didn't realize you'd become my social secretary, too.'

'Sounds like a wonderful trip, Jessica. I've been looking to get away for a week. It's been a hectic couple'a months at the office. I could use a week in that clean, crisp Colorado air, good, hearty home-cooked meals, songs around the campfire. I figured you'd enjoy those things, too.'

'I would, but—'

9

'Seems to me that saddling up a big, strong steed and ridden' him up into the rugged Colorado mountains would fit in just fine with your new need for adventure.'

'I haven't ridden a horse in . . . in a very long time.'

'How long a time?'

'Oh, thirty years. Maybe more.'

'You never forget.'

'But the horse might.'

He stood, stretched, and gave me a friendly smile. 'Of course, maybe riding tall in the saddle is a little too adventuresome for you.'

'Oh no, it's—'

'Have to run. Give Jim and Bonnie a call and let 'em know you'll be accompanying me. Think I'll mosey down to Charles Department Store and see what sort of duds they have. Maybe a Stetson hat and a red bandana.'

I couldn't help but laugh. 'Next thing I know you'll be singing like Roy Rogers and calling me ma'am.'

'Nothing of the sort—ma'am. Or should I say pardner?'

## CHAPTER TWO

By the time Seth and I were to leave for Colorado, I'd managed to squeeze in seven more flying lessons with Jed Richardson, giving me eight hours of dual instruction.

'Time for you to solo,' Jed said as he signed my log book following my eighth hour in the right seat.

'Solo? Me?'

'Right you are, Jess. You're ready.'

'Are you sure?'

He laughed. 'Wouldn't put you up there alone if I wasn't. The only difference will be a slight shift in weight with me out of the plane. Piece'a cake.'

I went home feeling both exuberant and apprehensive. Take the Cessna 172 up *alone*? I didn't share Jed's confidence in me. Jed told me that soloing after eight hours was the norm. But maybe I wasn't normal, at least when it came to flying a plane. Despite having become comfortable piloting the aircraft, my takeoffs and landings smooth, my in-air manoeuvres executed to Jed's satisfaction, the contemplation of taking the controls without him next to me was anathema. In a sense, the trip to Colorado would get me off the hook for a week, giving me time to think about whether I'd go through with a solo flight after only eight hours of instruction.

I expressed my concerns to Seth Hazlitt the day before we were to depart Cabot Cove for the Cooks' Powderhorn Guest Ranch. 'I just don't know if I can do it,' I told him as we sat in his office, enjoying tea and macaroons.

'Then *don't* do it,' he said. 'Just because

you've learned to fly a plane doesn't mean you have to fly it—alone. Thank Jed, and put the experience behind you.'

'I'll think about it,' I said. 'All set for the trip?'

'*Ayuh*. Everything's packed 'cept for a few last-minute things. You?'

'Getting there. I bought new jeans and a flannel jacket. I'm hoping to find a good pair of boots today.'

'Make sure they've got a good heel on them. Makes riding a horse easier.'

'I know. Bonnie made that point in the material she sent.'

'Talked to Jim last night. The man is as funny as ever. Always has a joke at the ready.'

I fondly recalled when Jim and Bonnie Cook lived in Cabot Cove. Jim's fondness for jokes, and his wonderful way of telling them, enlivened many a party.

'I'm really excited about the trip,' I said.

'Me, too. I'll confirm our flight before we leave.'

'As you always do. Have to run and look for those boots. Been practicing your western drawl?'

'*Ayuh*.'

'That's not western talk. That's pure Maine.'

'I'll work on it,' he said.

I eventually found my boots at Charles Department Store, where the owners, brothers

Jim and David, gave me their usual undivided attention. I went home from there to finish packing. Satisfied I'd included everything listed on my packing list—I'm an inveterate list-maker, especially when it comes to traveling—I settled in my study to again read the material Jim and Bonnie Cook had sent in advance of the trip. The more I read, the more enthusiastic I became, and wished Seth and I were already there, breathing in the clean Colorado air, and hearing Jim Cook's jokes again. It will be soon enough, I told myself as I chose a couple of books to take on the trip from a pile of recently purchased novels and biographies.

I'm an early-to-bed person. But on Saturday night I was under the covers even earlier than usual. Our flight to Denver from Bangor left at nine the next morning, which meant our hired car would be picking us up at five-thirty. Actually, we could have left an hour later, but Seth Hazlitt likes getting to airports early. *Very early.*

We were driven by Dimitri Cassis, a Greek immigrant who'd settled with his family in Cabot Cove after buying the local taxi company from Jake Monroe. Dimitri was a delightful, hard-working man who'd quickly expanded his taxi company to include a Lincoln Town Car, which he used to transport residents to points out of town. Because I don't drive, I use his services often, and have a house account. He'd driven me to my last three flying lessons and had stayed twice to watch me shoot landings and takeoffs under Jed Richardson's watchful tutelage. I actually saw Dimitri applauding after one particularly smooth landing, which made me smile, and feel even greater pride in my performance at the controls.

My experience piloting the controls of an aircraft, as brief and rudimentary as it might have been, caused me to view commercial aircraft and crews with a different eye. Silly as it may sound, I now felt one with them, and understood why they chose to spend their working lives in an airplane high above the earth.

As we boarded the large jet in Bangor, I paused to peek through the open cockpit door at the maze of dials and switches, and wanted to slip in there and sit in the captain's seat.

'Jessica, you're holding up traffic,' Seth said.

'What? Oh, sorry. I was daydreaming.'

'Appears you were. Let's take our seats.'

The flight was uneventful, and on time. My brief brush with piloting an aircraft gave me a different perspective on being a passenger. Although the huge jet was considerably more complex than my Cessna 172, the basic principles of flight are the same, and I took pleasure in understanding why the multi-ton jet was able to take off at all: the Bernouli principle at work.

A plane's wing is slightly curved on top, causing air moving over it to have to go faster than air moving beneath it. That's because, according to Mr. Bernouli's theory, the air flowing over both the top and bottom of a wing must arrive at the trailing edge at the same time. Faster-moving air exerts less pressure than slower-moving air. The increased pressure beneath the wing causes 'lift,' enabling the aircraft to break the proverbial bonds of earth and become airborne.

'What are you thinking about?' Seth asked.

I explained my understanding of the Bernouli theory to him.

'Didn't know that,' he said when I'd finished.

'See?' I said smugly. 'Look how much I'm learning by taking flying lessons.'

I spent the rest of the flight reading one of the books I'd packed. Before I knew it, we'd landed at Denver's sprawling new airport and were about to board a smaller aircraft for the forty-five-minute flight to Gunnison. Until learning how to fly, I never paid attention to the type of plane on which I was traveling. But I took note that we'd now be on a Mountain Air Express Dornier 328, a twin-engine turbo-prop craft with a row of narrow seats on either side of the passenger cabin. Seth had some trouble squeezing into his seat, but he managed, and we took off with a roar, flying

15

relatively low over the majestic Colorado terrain, multicolored desert giving way to pink canyons and redrock mountains. After a turn to the right, which brought us over the Sawatch Mountain Range, we landed on a very long runway for such a small airport. The captain reversed the pair of powerful engines to help us slow down, left the runway, and taxied to the small, functional terminal where Jim Cook, resplendent in jeans, blue denim shirt, boots, and a large Stetson hat, was waiting. Jim is a tall, handsome man with a twinkle in his eye and a smile always at the ready.

'Welcome,' he announced loudly as we approached. 'You two are a sight for sore eyes.'

I hugged him, and Seth energetically shook his hand. We gathered our luggage and went to the parking lot immediately outside the main entrance, where Jim had parked his large utility vehicle. I sat up front with him while Seth settled in the rear seat.

'How have you and Bonnie been?' I asked.

'Just fine,' he said, turning on to a road leading from the airport.

'Beautiful day,' Seth said.

'Typical,' Jim said. 'Starts off crisp and cool, but by the time you come out of breakfast, the sun's warmed things up nicely. Was below freezing when I got up. Must be sixty now.'

'Heavenly,' I said.

'Close as you can get,' said Jim. 'Of course, the winter can be rough. Some of the coldest temperatures ever recorded in the U.S. were recorded right here in Gunnison.'

The ride to the ranch took us through spectacular scenery, particularly along the perimeter of Blue Mesa, one of three reservoirs and Colorado's largest body of water. The state's reputation as a haven for outdoor sports enthusiasts was evident; people were camped all along the shoreline and in the low hills surrounding Blue Mesa, and the reservoir was dotted with boats of every description.

'Everyone seems so at peace,' I said.

'Colorado does that to you,' Jim said. 'A peaceful, idyllic paradise, as far as Bonnie and I are concerned. That's why people flock here on vacation, to get away from pollution and stress, crime and noise and rudeness.' He looked at me and laughed. 'After a week with us at the ranch, Jess, you'll be calling back to Cabot Cove to have somebody sell your house and ship your things out here.'

'Unlikely,' Seth said in his usual compact way.

I turned. 'Maybe more likely than you think.'

We ended up on a dirt road running along a river and past other ranches. Then the Powderhorn Ranch came into view. Jim turned into the property, waved at young men

17

and women working with horses in a corral, and came to a stop in front of the home Jim and Bonnie had built for themselves after buying the ranch. It also served as the office.

'Here we are,' Jim said, hopping out of the vehicle and coming around to help me down. Bonnie Cook came from the office. She, too, wore western clothing—jeans, blue denim shirt with fancy, colorful embroidery, and boots. She hadn't changed a bit since leaving Cabot Cove, petite and trim with a glowing smile. She embraced us, asked about our trip, and led us inside where she'd laid out a tea service and sandwiches.

'What a pretty home,' I said.

'Thanks,' Bonnie said, 'although it can use some sprucing up. Once the season starts, we just don't have time. But there's always the long winter.'

Jim drove the utility vehicle to our cabins and unloaded the luggage, while Bonnie escorted us on foot. All cabins at the Powderhorn were constructed of Ponderosa pine, and were identified either by the name of one of Santa's reindeers, or the seven dwarfs. The sign on my cottage read PRANCER. Seth's was a few cabins down the line and consisted of two attached units with doors leading to a common porch. It was called BLITZEN. All the porches were painted red.

Inside, my cabin was inviting and comfortable. There was a living room, two bedrooms, and a bath. A coffeemaker sat atop a small refrigerator.

'I'll leave you to get settled,' Jim Cook said.

'Has that family arrived yet?' I asked.

'The Morrisons? They're due here any minute, at least most of them. One of them—his name's Craig—the older son, I think, and very rich—arrives in his own plane.'

'Is there an airport in Powderhorn?'

'Just a little grass strip a few miles north. Craig Morrison owns a twin-engine jet, but the runway's not long enough to accommodate it. He flies his other plane, a Cessna.'

'I've been taking flying lessons,' I said proudly.

'You have? Last thing I'd think you'd be interested in doing.'

'Why?'

'Oh, I don't know. Just can't see you flying a plane.'

'Neither can Seth. Can you see me riding a horse?'

He laughed. 'I can see that very clearly. First thing in the morning. Well, you get settled, put your feet up and relax. Dinner's in the lodge at six-thirty. We'll introduce everybody before we sit down. Great seeing you and Doc Hazlitt again, Jess. Bonnie's thrilled you're here.'

I watched him saunter down the dirt road, meet up with Bonnie, who'd just come from Seth's cabin, and walk together to their home.

19

How wonderful, I thought, to have been able to fulfill a lifelong dream, in their case owning and operating a dude and guest ranch in the Colorado wilderness. So few people ever actually get to see their dreams realized. It couldn't have happened to nicer people.

While I was unpacking, it turned dark outside, and rain begin pelting the roof and windows. It was over in minutes, and the sun came out again. Powderhorn, Colorado, was obviously a place that gave credence to the adage that if you didn't like the weather, all you had to do was wait a few minutes for it to change.

A bottle of sparkling water had been placed in the cabin. I poured a glass and sat on the porch, watching dark storm clouds move swiftly along a high ridge, blocking the sun every few moments, then racing by to allow it to shine through.

Two long black limousines arrived while I sat there. They pulled up in front of the house/office, and their passengers went inside. The Morrison family, I assumed, ready to start its annual one-week reunion. As I watched the comings and goings, the sound of an aircraft engine captured my attention. I went to the railing and leaned out to be able to see beyond the roof's overhang. Sure enough, a Cessna 172, the same sort of aircraft in which I'd been taking lessons, approached from over Bonnie and Jim's house. It was low; I judged it to be no higher than two hundred feet. Its flaps were lowered, which said to me it was on its final approach to landing.

It passed directly in front of me, close enough for me to see the man at the controls, undoubtedly Craig Morrison, the wealthy, oldest son of the Morrison clan. It quickly disappeared from view.

Witnessing the arrival of Mr. Morrison at the controls of his own plane caused my heart to trip. Soon, I'd be back in Cabot Cove faced with the decision of whether to make my first solo flight. That contemplation was, at once, exciting and daunting.

Before leaving the cabin to join the others for dinner, I changed into my newly acquired western outfit. Satisfied with what I saw in the bedroom's full-length mirror, I stepped out onto the porch, took a deep breath of early evening air, smiled at the sound of horses neighing in the corral, heard a bell announcing it was dinnertime, and headed for the lodge, refreshed and relaxed, and happy to be there.


CHAPTER THREE

As I left my cabin and started across a grassy area separating the cabins from the main lodge, I was joined by one of Jim and Bonnie

Cook's two dogs, Socks, a black-and-white border collie who earned his keep by helping to herd the horses each night into the stables. He carried a stick in his mouth.

'Oh, no,' I said, remembering what Bonnie had told us over tea. A year ago, one of the guests had tossed a stick, which Socks dutifully retrieved. When the guest attempted to take the stick from Socks's mouth, the dog nipped the guest's finger. The guest was gracious about it, but Bonnie instituted a rule that guests were not to play catch with Socks.

'Go on, get away,' I said.

He followed me, the stick still in his mouth.

'No games,' I said. 'That's the rule.'

Socks spotted others heading for the lodge and ran to them in search of a playmate.

'Frisky little devil,' Seth said, coming up behind.

'So cute. Did you nap?'

'Didn't intend to, but dozed off for a spell. This change in altitude is hard on the breathing. You sleep?'

'No. I sat with my feet up on the porch and relaxed. Did you see the plane?'

'*Ayuh.* Damn fool pilot woke me up, flyin' so low.'

'It must have been Mr. Morrison.'

'I'll have a few words with him at dinner.'

'Now don't get yourself all *jo-jeezly* while we're here,' I said. Seth Hazlitt can become ornery at times. 'He won't be flying his plane

22

again until we leave.'

Bonnie and Jim stood with other people beneath an overhang in front of the lodge. Jim yelled, 'Jessica, Seth, come meet the Morrisons.'

We were introduced to four members of the family.

Chris Morrison, the younger of the two adult Morrison brothers, was a handsome young man with a boyish face. He wore clothing more appropriate to a Caribbean resort—white slacks, teal V-neck sweater over a blue button-down shirt, and alligator loafers, sans socks. I judged him to be in his early thirties. His wife, Marisa, was reed thin and as taciturn as her husband was gregarious.

'I've always wanted to meet you, Mrs. Fletcher,' Craig Morrison said, beaming as he shook my hand. 'You're my favorite writer.'

I graciously accepted what was undoubtedly an overstatement. I extended my hand to his wife, which she took tentatively. Her clothing was more befitting of a dude ranch vacation— blue jeans, tan riding boots, and a fleece-lined brown leather jacket over a white blouse.

The two other members of the Morrison family standing with the Cooks were teenagers. Pauline Morrison, we were told, was Craig Morrison's daughter, age fifteen, a pretty girl with red hair, large green eyes, and a crop of freckles splashed across her cheeks. Her brother, Godfrey, was sixteen. That they came from the same parents was surprising. Godfrey was dark-skinned. His hair was thick and black, and was cut into what seemed to be the fashion of the day, shaved a few inches above his ears, the top full and slicked back with some sort of gel. Pauline was outgoing and friendly; Godfrey was more the shy, brooding type.

'Ready for a hearty meal?' Jim Cook asked.

'I could use some dinner,' Seth said. 'Airline food wasn't much to write home about.'

'Well, let's get inside and see what Joel's whipped up for us this evening.' He turned to Chris Morrison. 'Where's the rest of the family?'

'Running late, as usual,' he replied. 'They'll be along shortly.'

I stopped to read a sign posted above a water fountain on the porch: FREE SOFT DRINKS—HELP YOURSELF.

Jim Cook's sense of humor on display, I thought, as I followed everyone inside.

The lodge consisted of two spacious rooms and a professionally equipped kitchen. The smaller of the two rooms, the one you entered from the outside, contained tables set for dinner. The kitchen was through a doorway on the back wall. A flashing, antique Seeburg jukebox dominated one corner of the dining room. 'Don't put any money in it,' Bonnie cautioned. 'Everything works except the music.'

Standing next to the jukebox was a bigger-than-life cardboard cut-out of John Wayne, dressed in a cowboy outfit and holding a carbine. Stuffed elk and deer heads observed everything from their vantage points on the walls. A large, glass-faced bookcase housed hundreds of books left behind by previous guests.

'I see a couple of your books, Jess,' Seth said after a quick perusal.

'We have all your books at the house,' Jim said. 'Come on, let me show you the new wing.'

We passed into an even larger room, where we were introduced to young wranglers and other ranch staff, whose friendliness and enthusiasm were contagious. The room contained a piano, pool table, tables piled with books and games, a huge projection TV system, a massive fireplace, and a dozen oversized lounge chairs. All the decorations had an Indian motif, with the exception of an autographed picture of the late, great comedian George Burns.

'Tomorrow night's movie night,' Jim announced. 'Every Monday. Plenty of western videos to choose from.'

We went to where the videos were lined up and immediately started a debate over which film we would watch the following night when the rest of the Morrison clan came through the door, led by Evelyn Morrison, a stunning,

25

patrician older woman who defined the term *matriarch*. Her youthful figure nicely filled out her tight-fitting designer jeans, silk plaid shirt and down vest. Her silver-blond hair was perfectly coiffed beneath a black Stetson studded with rhinestones, her makeup expertly applied to a smooth, slightly elongated, perfectly tanned face that was remarkably free of wrinkles. The immediate impression was a woman who took meticulous care of herself and was no stranger to personal pampering or plastic surgeons.

With her was the rest of the brood. Introductions established them as her oldest son, Craig, who'd flown in his own plane; Willy Morrison, who I would learn later was an unmarried cousin; and Robert Morrison, Evelyn's brother.

'This is the seventh year the Morrisons have held their reunion at Powderhorn,' Jim Cook announced.

'A lovely tradition,' I said to Evelyn Morrison. 'You're fortunate to be able to bring everyone together like this.'

'Family is everything,' she said haughtily. 'I would kill for my family.'

Her blunt, uncalled-for statement brought a moment of silence to the room. The staff and Jim and Bonnie left to get dinner moving. Once Evelyn was seated regally in a chair, the other Morrisons clustered about her and fell into conversation with one another, leaving

Seth and me pretty much on our own. We settled at the games table and were in the process of discovering what was on it when Craig Morrison came to us. He was a crudely handsome man, powerfully built, his face square and with a heavy beard line, his thick lips and perpetually furrowed brow creating a look that might be termed arrogant or menacing, and even cruel. At least that's how I would have described him as a character in one of my novels.

'Jim Cook says you're taking flying lessons, Mrs. Fletcher,' he said.

'That's right. I saw you arrive this afternoon in your plane. I'm flying a Cessna 172, too. Well, I suppose I shouldn't say I'm flying one. I'm scheduled to make my first solo flight when I get back to Maine.' I glanced at Seth, who raised his eyebrows and sighed.

'First solo flight, huh? I made mine a long time ago. I was a teenager.'

'I understand you also fly a more sophisticated business jet, Mr. Morrison.'

'That's right. You a pilot, too, Doctor?'

'Nope. Just as soon have somebody else fly me where I'm going.'

Morrison ignored Seth and said to me, 'Let's find a few hours this week to do some flying together.'

'Oh, I don't think I'm up to that.'

'I'll put you through the paces, get you ready for your solo.'

27

'Well, maybe. We'll see how the week goes. And please call me Jessica.'

Jim Cook appeared in the doorway. 'Dinner is served.'

I was pleasantly surprised that the ranch's staff ate with the guests. At other resorts at which I'd been a guest, staff was segregated at mealtimes. Having the ebullient young people at the table livened things up considerably. The cook, Joel Louden, was slightly older than the rest but not by much. He verbally gave us the evening's menu: barbecue beef brisket, homemade potato salad and bread, baked beans, a salad of pickled vegetables, and banana cream pie for dessert. I was glad I hadn't bought tight clothing for the trip. You leave your diets at home when visiting a western dude ranch.

'Take your vitamin E,' Bonnie said, pointing to a large bottle of the vitamin on the table. 'It'll help you acclimate to the altitude change.'

Seth eagerly opened the bottle and washed one down with water.

'Do you know what you call a dog with no legs?' Jim Cook asked as plates were placed in front of us.

Seth and I looked at each other, remembering that Jim always set up a joke by asking a question. 'What do you call a dog with no legs, Jim?' we asked in unison, playing the game.

'Nothing. He won't come anyway.'

The laughter was interrupted by the sound of a car passing the lodge. Bonnie stood and said, 'That must be the Molloys.'

'Who are the Molloys?' Evelyn Morrison asked from where she sat at one end of the table.

'Guests,' Bonnie said. 'A last-minute booking. We have one vacant cabin and—'

'We were to have the ranch to ourselves,' Evelyn said sternly.

'We told you Mrs. Fletcher and Dr. Hazlitt would be here,' Jim said.

'Which we agreed to,' said Craig, the older son.

'Nice folks, the Molloys,' Jim said, smiling. 'Really wanted to come this week, couldn't make it any other week. Fairly begged for us to take them. So, we did.' He looked up at one of the girls serving dinner. 'I'd appreciate another biscuit, Sue.'

As Bonnie left to check in the later arrivals, I silently complimented Jim on taking his subtle stand with the Morrisons. As gracious a host and hostess as Jim and Bonnie were, they also obviously ran the ranch in a way that satisfied their needs, too.

Bonnie returned with the Molloys as dessert was being served. She introduced them and said two extra dinners had been saved for them. 'Joel, our cook, had to take the rest of the night off. Something about seeing a friend in Gunnison. But he made sure to whip up two

29

extra dinners.' Room was made, and they joined us at the table.

'The Molloys are from Nevada,' Bonnie said. 'They're on a driving tour of the Rocky Mountain area.'

'What do you do for a living, Mr. Molloy?' Evelyn Morrison asked bluntly.

Paul Molloy was a beefy, middle-aged man with a ruddy face and gray hair the consistency of steel wool. 'Land management,' he replied, seemingly not offended by the rudeness of the question.

'In Nevada?' Evelyn asked.

'And elsewhere,' Molloy said, taking a bite of a biscuit. His wife, Geraldine, was no taller than five feet. Her nose and cheekbones were sharply chiseled, the look of someone who takes exercising seriously, perhaps too seriously. They ate their dinners and had little to say for the rest of the meal. When asked by Jim whether they'd be riding in the morning, Mrs. Molloy said, 'Maybe in a day or two. I think we'll just relax tomorrow.'

'Suit yourself,' Jim said.

The Morrison children, Godfrey and Pauline, bolted from the table immediately following dessert, and the other family members, with the exception of Cousin Willy, drifted away. Jim explained to Willy, Seth, and me that he needed to get a sense of our experience with horses in order to choose the right mount for each of us. Willy was the only

Morrison who hadn't been to the ranch before; the others' horses had been chosen long ago. The ranch's chief wrangler, Joe Walker, had remained at the table to help Jim decide which horses were appropriate for the group's tenderfoots.

Willy was a nervous fellow, eyes always in motion, his hands engaged in a variety of gestures. He was in his late thirties, I surmised, and he did not share the rest of the family's healthy, robust appearance. He was a slight man who'd balded prematurely, the expanse of bare skin made more evident by the irregular, bumpy surface of his head. Wearing a suit and tie to dinner had prompted a few amusing comments.

'Horses scare me,' Willy said.

Jim laughed. 'Nothing to be afraid of,' he said. 'Have you had a bad experience with a horse before?'

'No.'

'They're as gentle as they're treated,' Jim said. 'We'll pair you up with a nice easy horse, teach you a few simple tricks in the morning, and you'll get along just fine.' He turned to me. 'Been riding much lately, Jess?'

'No. It's been years.'

'You, Doc?'

'Not afraid of horses, Jim, but haven't been in the saddle in a long time.'

'We'll take that into account, won't we, Joe?'

31

Walker, an amiable, enthusiastic young man with clear, sparkling eyes and a sweet, perpetual smile, said, 'That's what's good about having so many horses. There's a perfect one for every rider.' He handed us cards to fill out, which contained spaces for our height and weight.

'Do we have to say how much we weigh?' I asked pleasantly.

'At least we're not asking for your age,' Jim said. 'Knowing your height and weight helps Joe pick the right horse for you.'

We filled out the cards, thanked Jim for a wonderful meal, and Seth and I went outside.

'Feel like a walk?' I asked.

'Not a long one. I'm looking forward to getting to bed early.'

We looked up. Night-time heavens in Maine can be startlingly clear, but I'd never seen anything like the Colorado sky. Billions of distinct stars were highlighted against a black scrim, like diamonds on black velvet.

'Puts us in perspective, doesn't it?' I said.

'*Ayuh*. Nature always does.'

We strolled down the road, the sound of Cebolla Creek, a fast-moving trout stream that ran directly through the ranch, providing pleasant, gurgling background sounds. I'd brought a four-piece Hardy fly rod, lightweight wading boots and waders, and an assortment of my favorite artificial flies. I love fly fishing and do as much of it back home as time permits. Trout fishing in Colorado was worthy of legends, I'd been told, and I intended to find some fishing time on the creek each day.

We crossed a red footbridge over a narrow stream that fed a stocked trout pool, to a private island on the banks of the Cebolla, where barbecues were held, and where we would sit around a campfire later in the week swapping stories and, according to Bonnie, be entertained by Andy, one of the wranglers, who played guitar and sang.

'It's so lovely here,' I said.

'Peaceful,' Seth said. He drew a deep breath.

I shivered and verbally expressed the chill I suddenly felt.

'Time to get back to the cabins,' Seth said. 'No sense catchin' a cold first day here.'

'It is chilly,' I said, 'but there's something else.'

'Which is?' he asked as we retraced our steps toward the lodge.

'The Morrison family. Do you get the feeling that all isn't well among them?'

'Strange bunch, I agree. Not an especially happy group.'

'The mother, Evelyn, is a cold woman.'

'That she is. Seems to run the family with an iron fist.'

'The kids seem nice.'

'The girl, maybe. The boy looks like he's brimmin' over with anger.'

We crossed the grassy area, causing us to pass other cabins. As we did, voices from one—angry voices—spilled through the slightly open window.

'She'll be here tomorrow,' a man said. I recognized the voice as belonging to Craig Morrison, the older son. Seth and I paused.

'What was so important that she had to stay in Denver an extra day?'

'You know Veronica, Mother. She always has to be different.'

'I don't like it, Craig.'

'You don't like *her*, Mother.'

'What's to like? How you could have married her is beyond me. You barely knew her.'

'You know damn well why I married her. It seemed like a good idea at the time, for me and for you.'

'It was a mistake. I've never trusted her.'

'I'll keep tabs on her, make sure nothing goes wrong.'

Seth tugged on my sleeve. I nodded. We were eavesdropping, not an especially noble activity. But as we started to leave, Evelyn Morrison said, 'Tell me more about this Molloy.'

'I don't know, Mother. I just have this feeling I've met him, or at least know something about him. I have a call in to Rick Swales. I'll know more when he gets back to me.'

Seth and I said good night in front of his cabin.

'Seems the Morrisons have more on their minds than a relaxing week at a dude ranch,' Seth said.

'My thoughts exactly. Well, it's none of our business. All that's on my mind is a relaxing week at the Powderhorn Ranch. Good night, Seth. Sleep tight.'

'You, too, Jessica. Morning will be here before we know it.'

## CHAPTER FOUR

I was up at dawn and took a brisk walk around the property. It had rained hard during the night; the grass and dirt trails were wet. The wranglers were already at work in the stables, grooming the horses, putting out their feed, cleaning mud from their hooves, and performing the seemingly hundred other chores that go with being a wrangler.

I showered and dressed for the day, then whiled away the time till breakfast on the porch, reading the book I'd started on the flight to Denver, a sweater wrapped tightly around me to ward off the morning chill. I hadn't felt the altitude yesterday, but by the time I returned from my walk, I'd decided to add vitamin E to the breakfast menu.

Craig Morrison jogged past and returned my greeting with a cursory nod. Members of the ranch's staff pleasantly went about their duties, waving when they spotted me, stopping to chat now and then when passing my cabin. Before I knew it, it was seven-thirty, and Jim was ringing the bell announcing it was time for a half hour of coffee before breakfast.

'All set for a nice ride this morning?' Bonnie asked as we sat down for blueberry pancakes, sausage links, and cherry rings. Bonnie and Jim serve dessert at every meal, breakfast no exception. Everyone was there, except for the Molloys.

'She looks like she eats only one meal a week,' Chris Morrison said of Geraldine Molloy, laughing.

'Not good to skip breakfast,' Seth offered, 'especially with a strenuous day ahead.'

'We'll have a half-hour lesson in the corral,' Jim said. 'Then we'll head off. One of the wranglers will lead a short ride into the lower hills, ease you into it. Those with more experience will go higher up. Let me get some video of you.' He produced an elaborate camcorder and panned the table, explaining that he'd be videotaping us all week, the finished movie to be shown after dinner the following Saturday.

We went directly to the corral after breakfast, where the wranglers awaited our arrival, along with the two ranch dogs, Socks, with his usual stick in his mouth, and Holly, a caramel-and-white mixed breed, only slightly more docile than her frenetic brother. Their paws were covered with mud, as our shoes and boots would soon be.

The only female wrangler, Crystal Kildare, stood holding the reins of a fine-looking chestnut mare. Despite having dressed in what I thought was authentic western gear, I felt very much the city slicker in the company of the wranglers, who looked as though they were born in their jeans and shirts, boots and broad-brimmed hats.

'Good morning,' Crystal said. 'Everybody well fed and ready to ride?'

Evelyn Morrison, her older son, Craig, and Craig's son, Godfrey, stood apart from the group, boredom written all over their faces. Next to me was Craig's daughter, Pauline, who was intensely interested in what Crystal was about to say. Willy Morrison stood a few feet behind us. He'd discarded his suit jacket and tie, but wore a white shirt, suit pants, and high-top white sneakers. One of the wranglers told him that riding in sneakers wasn't a good idea, and found him a pair of boots from the ranch's sizable collection.

As we waited for Crystal to begin her instructions, my attention was drawn to Robert Morrison, Evelyn's brother. It was as though he'd been absent at dinner and breakfast, despite having been there physically. I judged him to be about ten years younger than his sister. He shared Evelyn's intensity, particularly in the eyes. Their faces, sharp and angular, further testified to their common parentage. But what bound them together as a family—all except Pauline—was a look of anger and suspicion, disdain and sourness.

'This is Daisy,' Crystal said. 'She's my horse while I'm at Powderhorn. There are a few basic things you should know about horses. First, they don't see straight ahead. They only have peripheral vision, so always approach them from the side, not from the front. And there's a proper way to mount. Let me demonstrate.'

She placed her left foot in the stirrup, reached up, grabbed a handful of the horse's mane, and pulled herself up and over. Once in the saddle, she said, 'Notice how I used the mane, not the saddle horn? If you use the saddle horn, you're shifting the saddle, which you don't want to do. Using the mane doesn't hurt the horse and gives you a better grip when mounting. Now, let me show you a few ways to get your horse to go where you want it to go.'

I smiled as she put Daisy through its paces. Crystal was a tall, attractive young woman who was supremely confident in the saddle as she turned her horse left and right, then made a complete circle using the reins and gentle pressure from her knees. She explained verbally what she was doing while performing the exercise. Jim Cook videotaped us, and Pauline Morrison took pictures with a small point-and-shoot camera.

Crystal brought Daisy to where we stood and said, 'Take all the pictures you want while we're on our ride, but don't use the last shot on the roll. Most cameras have an automatic rewind once the final picture has been taken. That noise tends to spook horses.'

'Interesting,' Seth said.

'I'm excited,' I said.

The other wranglers brought our horses from the stables. Mine was a lovely midsized black steed named Samantha. Seth's horse, Blazer, was the biggest horse on the ranch. I glanced at Seth. His eyes were wide, his forehead furrowed.

'He's a big one,' I said.

'*Ayuh*. Long way to fall.'

'But you won't be falling.'

Crystal positioned a step stool next to Blazer and invited Seth to use it to help him mount. We watched as my dear friend, caring physician, and civic leader struggled valiantly to follow Crystal's advice and haul his corpulent self up on Blazer. It took a few tries, but suddenly he was in the saddle and looking as though he belonged there, his Stetson pulled low over his eyes like a character in a western shoot-em-up.

'Something else to remember,' Crystal said. 'Never wrap the reins around the saddle horn.

And when you get off your horse to walk him, don't wrap it around your hand. If he should decide to take off, you don't want to be dragged behind.'

Soon everyone was on their chosen horses, and we split into two groups, the more experienced riders to follow wrangler Andy Wilson into the higher elevations, and my group of inexperienced riders who would accompany Crystal on a less challenging ride.

Ten minutes later, the experienced group left the road and veered onto a rutted dirt trail leading up into the mountains. We continued on the flat surface until Crystal led us up a moderate rise leading into the lower foothills.

We proceeded at a leisurely pace, a slow walk. Seth was directly behind Crystal, who glanced back at regular intervals to make sure all was well with her tenderfoot contingent. The rules at the Powderhorn were strict, with safety always uppermost in mind. Jim and Bonnie belonged to the Colorado Dude and Guest Ranch Association, whose book of safety regulations was as thick as one of my novels.

Although it was barely ten o'clock, the sun had heated the air, which in turn coaxed insects out of their cool homes. Seth repeatedly wiped his face with the red bandana he'd bought especially for the trip and frequently looked back to see that I was okay. I did the same with Willy Morrison. He was slumped in his saddle, his face reflecting his unhappiness. Why, I wondered, had he bothered coming to the ranch in the first place? And he didn't have to ride a horse. Bonnie had told me that a number of guests come for reasons other than riding. In one case she recounted, a woman, dressed in expensive cowboy clothing, mounted a horse after the briefing, instructed her husband to take a picture, then immediately climbed down and never went near a horse again.

After forty-five minutes, Crystal brought the column to a halt and suggested we dismount and stretch a little before heading back. We'd climbed higher than I'd realized. The plateau was surrounded by groves of aspen trees and ponderosa pines. From it the views were lovely, mountains providing a rugged backdrop for rolling meadows and pastures. A hawk circled overhead in the cobalt Colorado sky; chipmunks scurried from fallen tree to fallen tree, and two deer watched impassively from a safe distance. Wildflowers set the hills ablaze with color.

'The Molloys never did show up,' Seth said, arching his back against an ache that had developed.

'I hope they're all right,' I said.

Willy sat on the ground and propped himself against a tree. He was pale and breathing hard, his white shirt stained with perspiration.

41

'You all right, young fella?' Seth asked, standing over him.

Willy looked up. 'Yeah, I'm all right,' he said. 'Damn horse doesn't know how to walk right.'

Crystal heard him and laughed. 'Takes some getting used to,' she said. 'And some horses do walk different than others.'

We drank from canteens provided by the ranch, then got ready to head back. Socks continued to try to entice one of us to play fetch, but we didn't take the bait. Holly had a different game to play, which didn't depend upon human involvement. She enjoyed tearing through brush in pursuit of chipmunks and other small furry animals.

We started down to the road.

'Getting used to this,' Seth said, smiling.

'I know,' I said. 'A little sore, but it's worth it.'

We were almost to the road when Willy asked us to stop.

'What's the matter?' Crystal asked.

'I can't take this anymore,' he said, sliding down off his mount.

'You can walk him back,' Crystal said. 'But remember what I said. Don't wrap the reins around your hand.'

'I'll remember,' he grunted.

Crystal reached the road and waited for us to catch up. We started back to the ranch, meandering along, taking in the scenery and enjoying the moment. We'd just turned onto the short road leading into the ranch when Socks and Holly burst through some low brush in pursuit of a rabbit. Socks, carrying his customary stick, quickly lost interest in the chase. He came to Willy and offered him the stick. Willy pulled it from his mouth.

'You're not supposed to do that,' Crystal said.

Willy ignored her and tossed the stick over a row of bushes lining the road. Socks tore after it. Holly, who'd been outrun by the rabbit, joined him.

We all laughed at their antics, then prodded the horses to move again. We'd gone maybe another hundred feet and were within fifty yards of the lodge when the dogs' barking caused Crystal to halt the column and to look back at the canine commotion.

'They're sure excited about something,' Seth said.

Crystal turned Daisy and urged her through a break in the bushes. Socks and Holly continued to bark. We watched as Crystal dismounted and used her foot to part the brush. Suddenly, her scream filled our ears.

I slid down off Samantha, handed the reins to Seth, and ran to where Crystal stood, her face etched with shock.

'What is it?' I asked.

'Look.' She pointed.

I took a few steps in that direction and

leaned over to see what had caused her reaction. The lower portion of a leg protruded from beneath the underbrush. At the bottom of it was a brown, ankle-high man's hiking boot. A bit of white athletic sock protruded from it. There was a four-inch expanse of bare leg between where the sock stopped and the cuff of blue pants began. Burrs from low-lying bushes were stuck to his sock.

'My God,' I said.

'Who is it?' Crystal asked.

'What's the matter?' Seth shouted from his horse.

I drew a deep breath, closed my eyes, opened them, and used my hands to part the bushes. It took a moment to clear a visual path, but when I did, I recoiled as though bitten by a snake.

'Who is it?' Crystal repeated.

'It's Mr. Molloy,' I said. 'I'm afraid he's very dead.'


## CHAPTER FIVE

'I think someone should stay with the body,' I said, 'while we go tell Jim and Bonnie.'

'I will,' Crystal said, her voice reflecting her ambivalence.

I returned to where Seth and Willy Morrison waited.

44

'What's going on?' Seth asked.

'Mr. Molloy's body is over there.'

'Molloy? An accident?'

'It doesn't look that way to me, but that's something for the police to decide. Come on. We'd better let Jim and Bonnie know. Coming, Mr. Morrison?'

Willy was immobile; he looked frightened, in shock. He glanced back at Crystal, who'd retreated from Molloy's body and stood with her hand covering her mouth. He looked at me, dropped his horse's reins, and ran toward the cabins. I picked up the extra set of reins, and Seth and I walked the three horses to the house.

Joe Walker, the chief wrangler, came from the office as we approached. 'Good morning,' he said, tapping his wide-brimmed black hat. 'How was the ride?'

'The ride was fine,' Seth said. 'Not a happy ending, though.'

Walker's expression turned serious. 'Was someone hurt?'

'Someone's dead,' I said. 'Mr. Molloy.'

'An accident? Was he thrown?'

'I don't think so,' I said. 'He wasn't with us. Crystal discovered the body. She's staying with it.'

'Oh, boy,' Walker said. 'Do Jim and Bonnie know?'

'We're on our way to tell them. Would you take these horses back to their stables?'

'Sure.'

Bonnie was in the office, doing paperwork. ' 'Morning,' she said.

'Bonnie, something terrible has happened,' I said. 'We found Mr. Molloy's body on our way back from the ride.'

Jim came through the door from the house as I broke the news. 'Molloy? Found his body? What happened?'

'I don't know,' I said, 'but you'd better call the local police.'

'Where is he?' Bonnie asked.

Seth gave a rough description of where we'd discovered him.

'Let's go,' Jim said. 'Call the sheriff, Bonnie. I'll get a couple of wranglers to stand watch until he arrives.'

We followed Jim out of the office and up the road to where Crystal continued her lonely sentry duty. We stood with her as Jim parted the bushes and took a close look at Molloy. I came to his side. Molloy was on his back. From what I could see, he'd been stabbed or shot in the chest. A dark, crusty ring of blood dominated the center of the yellow shirt he wore. If he had been stabbed, the assailant had removed the instrument of death.

'The blood has crusted,' I said. 'It didn't just happen.'

'Last night?' Jim asked.

I shrugged. 'Hard to say. A medical examiner will make that determination.'

Jim said to Crystal, 'Go get a couple of other wranglers. I want to make sure nobody disturbs the scene. Am I right, Jess?'

'Oh, yes. That's important. You haven't touched anything, have you, Crystal?'

'No. I never got any closer than this.'

'Good.'

Crystal took off at a trot toward the stables.

'Is there a police force in Powderhorn?' Seth asked.

'No,' Jim said. 'The Gunnison County sheriff's office covers Powderhorn. It's a good force. Right up to date on all the new techniques and procedures.'

'That's good to hear,' I said.

While we waited, the Morrison family, led by Andy Wilson, came down the road.

'Howdy,' Andy said.

'Hello, Andy,' Jim said. He went to the road, motioned for Andy to join him away from the others, and whispered in the young wrangler's ear. You didn't have to hear Jim's words to know what he'd said. Andy's expression said it all. Obviously, Jim had instructed him to get the Morrisons away from the scene, and to not tell them what had happened.

'Let's move on,' Andy said.

Two other wranglers, Jon Adler and Toby Winters, joined us.

'You two stay here,' Jim said after filling them in on why they were there. 'Keep your

47

distance. If anybody comes by, pretend you're picking berries or something. Don't let anybody near the body.' We started back to the house when Jim stopped in the road, crouched, and examined a set of fresh tire marks in the wet dirt.

'Recent,' I said.

'Yes.'

'Did you see or hear a car or truck come by last night?' I asked.

'No. We don't get much traffic here. Days can go by without a car coming by. It's a car tire.'

We went to the house, where Bonnie waited in front, anxiety written all over her pretty face. 'The sheriff's out investigating a crime,' she said, 'but they're sending some of his deputies.'

'Good. They say how long it would be?'

'As fast as it takes to drive from Gunnison.'

'I can't believe this,' Jim said, more to himself than to us. 'In the fifteen years we've had the Powderhorn, we've never had anything serious happen before.' He turned to Bonnie. 'What, that broken leg ten years ago? Some scrapes and bruises? One heart attack, and that guest survived, did just fine. He came back the next year. We hear from him all the time.'

'It has nothing to do with you and the ranch,' I said.

'But it happened here.' Jim said.

'It had to be somebody passing through,' Bonnie said, 'a stranger, some itinerant drifter.'

'Where's Mrs. Molloy?' I asked.

We looked at each other. Geraldine Molloy had been forgotten in all that had transpired.

'Must be in her cabin,' Bonnie said. 'I'll go see.'

'Would you like me to go?' I asked.

'I don't want to intrude on you, Jess.'

'Don't give it a second thought. What cabin are the Molloys in?'

'The honeymoon cabin,' Jim said.

'Which is that?' I asked.

'The last cabin, just beyond yours, Jess.'

'Up on that little rise?'

'Right.'

'And no one has seen her?' Seth asked.

A shake of heads all around.

'I'll be back,' I said.

The Morrison clan, fresh from their morning ride, stood around the swimming pool, coffee cups in hand. I said hello as I passed, receiving less than enthusiastic responses. But they weren't on my mind at the moment. I was curious why Geraldine Molloy hadn't been seen all morning. Wasn't she aware that her husband wasn't with her? If my snap analysis was correct, that the crusted blood on his chest indicated he'd been killed some time during the night, it meant he'd left her alone in their cabin. Unless, of course, she'd been with him.

Why had he been out on the road at night? Trouble sleeping and took a walk? Always possible. A fight with his wife, causing him to storm out of the cabin? That was another possibility.

There was a sign on the front of the ranch's honeymoon cabin, white lettering on dark brown wood: THIS CABIN WAS THE FIRST LOVE NEST FOR OUR HAPPY HONEYMOONERS. Below was a list of honeymoon couples, and the dates they'd stayed there to launch their married life. Had the reason for my visiting it not been so grim, I might have had a warmer reaction to the sentiment.

I stood at the door and poised to knock. After a deep breath, I did. Both the screen and inside doors were closed. I looked at the front window. The curtains were drawn. I knocked again. Still no response.

'Mrs. Molloy?' I called. I repeated it, louder this time, accompanied by more knocking. I cocked my head; someone was moving inside.

'Mrs. Molloy, it's Jessica Fletcher.'

I looked at the interior doorknob as it started to turn, then stopped, as though whoever was turning it—Geraldine Molloy, I presumed—had second thoughts.

'Mrs. Molloy, it's Jessica—'

The inside door opened, revealing Geraldine Molloy. She was in pajamas. Her

50

reddish hair was disheveled, her eyes puffy with sleep.

'What do you want?' she asked in a thick voice.

'I need to talk to you,' I said.

'Come back later. You woke me.'

'I'm sorry to have done that, but it's important, Mrs. Molloy. There's been an . . . an accident. Your husband. He's . . . he's dead.'

From what I could observe through the screen, her expression didn't change.

'Did you hear me, Mrs. Molloy?'

Was she drugged? I wondered. Had she taken a potent sleeping pill that caused her to sleep so late and to be in a fog?

Then the news seemed to sink in. She uttered a small involuntary gasp and backed away from the door.

'Mrs. Molloy, I—'

She disappeared from my sight, and the sound of a door slamming reached me on the porch. I pulled on the screen door's handle. It wasn't latched. I opened it and stuck my head into the cabin. A closed door was to my right, obviously a bedroom into which she'd retreated. I took in the living room without stepping farther inside. It was in disarray. Clothing seemed to have been tossed about, draped over chair backs and on the floor. I crossed the threshold and silently closed the screen door behind me, then cocked my head to hear sounds from the bedroom. There were none. I crossed the living room to the area where the small refrigerator and coffeemaker were located. The coffeemaker was on, the carafe full. I touched the carafe; it was hot.

I wasn't sure what to do next. Should I knock on the bedroom door, call her name? Or would that have been an unwarranted intrusion into the shock and grief she must have been feeling at the moment? Maybe I shouldn't have volunteered to be the one to break the news. Perhaps we should have waited for the sheriff's deputy to arrive, someone more skilled at handling such delicate matters.

I decided to leave the cabin and sit on the porch for a few minutes to wait for her to pull herself together and emerge from her bedroom refuge. I was halfway across the living room when the sound of a door opening stopped me. I turned to face the bedroom. Geraldine Molloy stepped from it. She still wore pajamas, and her expression had not changed. What *was* different was that she held a lethal-looking handgun, and it was pointed at me.

I held out both hands as I said, 'Mrs. Molloy, there's no need for a gun. I'm not here to threaten you. I came to break bad news, and I wish I wasn't the one to do it. Please, put the gun down.'

'Paul is dead?'

'Yes. An accident. Well, maybe—the sheriff

52

is on his way now. Until he arrives, we must stay calm. Put the gun down, Mrs. Molloy. We can sit and talk until he's here.'

Until that moment, she'd been rock steady, not even a minute tremor in her hand. But now she began to shake, the weapon whipping back and forth. I was afraid it would discharge accidentally. I moved to my right, came closer to her, placed my hand on the gun, and took it from her. My heart was pounding, and perspiration dripped from my forehead down my nose. I drew a deep sigh of relief, placed the gun on a table, and went to her, my arms wrapped around her, allowing her to cry it out, her thin body heaving against me.

As I held her, I heard footsteps on the porch. I turned to see Jim Cook and Seth Hazlitt at the door.

'Everything okay?' Seth asked.

'Yes. Everything's fine. Why don't we give Mrs. Molloy a few extra minutes alone. I'm sure she'd like to freshen up and get dressed before the sheriff's people arrive.' I held her at arm's length. 'That would be a good idea, wouldn't it, Mrs. Molloy?'

'Yes,' she managed in a tiny voice. 'Yes, I'd like to do that.'

'I'll wait out on the porch.'

Before joining Seth and Jim on the porch, I quietly picked up the gun from the table and carried it with me, closing both doors behind me.

'How'd she take it?' Seth asked.

'Badly.' I held up the revolver.

'Where did you get that?' Jim asked.

'From her.'

'She threaten you with it, Jessica?' Seth asked.

'No. I'm sure she didn't mean to use it. It was nothing more than a reflex action born of fear and the devastating news I'd delivered.'

But I did silently admit to myself that her reaction was unusual, something I might follow up with her at a more opportune moment.

Jim used a handkerchief to place the weapon in his jacket pocket. 'I'll turn this over to the sheriff when he gets here. I'm sure he'll want to have it checked for prints.'

'Any word from him?' I asked.

'His on-duty road officer called in from the car,' Jim said. 'Talked to Bonnie. Should be here in ten, fifteen minutes. He's got the county coroner with him, and a homicide investigator. They've dispatched an ambulance, too, to remove the body, I suppose. Not much more to be done for Mr. Molloy.'

'Poor woman,' I said, referring to Geraldine. 'Have the Morrisons been told?'

'Yes,' Jim said. 'Felt I had to before they heard a rumor and started sensing something was wrong. Thought it was better to hear it directly from me, but the cousin, Willy, had

54

already told them.'

'What will this do to the week, Jim?' Seth asked.

'Bonnie and I had a brief talk about that,' Jim replied. 'Of course, we don't know what the sheriff will want from us and the guests, but if the investigation isn't too intrusive, we'd like to go on with the week as normally as possible, if that is possible. Bonnie's convinced that if it was murder, it had nothing to do with anybody here at the ranch. Some sickie passing through.'

'I hope that's the case,' I said. 'If it isn't—'

'I'd rather not think about that,' Jim said.

The door opened, and Geraldine came onto the porch. She'd obviously taken a fast shower; her hair was still wet. She was dressed in a simple blue denim dress and white cardigan sweater.

'Sorry about the news, Mrs. Molloy,' Jim said.

'I can't believe it,' she said. 'Paul dead? It's inconceivable. What happened? Did he fall off a horse? Was he kicked?'

'We don't know yet, ma'am. The police are on the way. Coroner, too.'

The word *coroner* caused Geraldine to shudder and to grip the porch railing for support.

'Why don't you sit down, Mrs. Molloy,' Seth suggested, pulling a chair closer to her. She sat, closed her eyes, and slowly shook her

55

head.

'Would you like some water?' Seth asked. 'Coffee? I'll get some from the lodge.'

'No need for that,' I said. 'There's coffee brewing in the cabin.'

Geraldine opened her eyes. 'There is?' she asked.

'Yes. Didn't you put it up?'

'No, Paul must have before he left this morning.'

'You know for certain he left this morning?' I asked.

'No. I just assumed he did.'

I stopped myself from saying that judging from what I'd seen of the body, Paul Molloy had been killed last night. But that was pure speculation on my part.

We all turned in the direction of the house, where two vehicles kicked up dust as they turned in to the ranch, lights flashing. One was a marked Gunnison County sheriff's car. The other was the ambulance. 'We'd better get over there,' Jim said.

'You go ahead,' I suggested. 'Seth and I will stay with Mrs. Molloy until she's needed.'

Jim took purposeful strides to the house. From where we stood, we could see that the vehicles had carried a number of people; we counted three in police uniforms, and the ambulance discharged a man and a woman wearing white—emergency medical personnel was the assumption.

I fetched Geraldine Molloy coffee from inside. As I poured it into a cup—she took it plain black—I paused to ponder what she'd said. If she was to be believed, and I had no reason not to, her husband had put up the pot. But when? It was unlikely he would have done that if he'd left during the night. And if my preliminary analysis was correct, he hadn't been there in the morning to do it.

'Here you are,' I said, handing the steaming cup to Mrs. Molloy.

She seemed to have relaxed and gave me a smile. 'Thank you,' she said. 'You're very kind.' She was certainly not the gun-wielding woman I'd first encountered when coming to the cabin to break the news of her husband's death. I preferred this version.

We watched Jim lead the entourage from the house to where the body was being guarded by the two wranglers.

'I think I'll join them,' I said. 'Mind staying with Mrs. Molloy, Seth?'

'No need for anyone to stay with me,' she said, standing. 'I'll be fine. I'd like to be there, too.'

'I don't think that's wise,' Seth said. 'Maybe we can stay in the house with Bonnie.'

'Good idea,' I said.

I walked with them to where Bonnie stood outside the office, her face set in anguish. 'Mrs. Molloy and Seth will stay here with you, Bonnie,' I said.

I went to where the others now surrounded the body. A uniformed officer stopped me.

'It's okay,' Jim Cook said. 'This is Jessica Fletcher, the famous mystery writer. She's a guest at the ranch this week. She was one of the people who found him.'

They'd cleared away the brush, leaving Paul Molloy's body exposed. The coroner was on his knees examining it, fingers gently probing certain areas. Molloy's eyes were open. Years of research into homicide investigations for my crime novels had taught me plenty, including that upon death the muscles controlling the pupils relax, causing them to lose the symmetrical appearance characteristic of being alive. His eyelids had become flabby, another sure sign of death.

The coroner, a large, beefy man wearing slacks, a yellow V-neck sweater over a white shirt, and elaborately tooled cowboy boots, continued his physical examination of the corpse. I knew what he was attempting to determine: the approximate time of death. He took Molloy's chin and carefully moved it from side to side, checking the level of rigor mortis that had set in. It starts simultaneously throughout the body, but progresses fastest in the jaws and neck. Generally, it begins three to four hours after death, progresses from the head down to the feet, and reaches its full effect between eight and twelve hours following death. I couldn't tell from where I stood what point of rigor had developed, but I had the sense it was pretty far along. If this coroner followed standard procedure, Molloy's temperature would be taken once he'd been delivered to the county morgue to further help establish time of death, an inexact measurement because of all the variables—size and weight of the deceased, environmental factors at the time of death, clothing, and myriad other factors to be taken into account.

One of the officers took multiple photographs of the body and the surroundings in which it had been found, while the other two searched the ground for clues that might have been left by an assailant.

'Can we move him?' the coroner asked the plainclothes homicide investigator, who'd been making notes.

'Yeah. We've got it all, I think.' He turned to Jim Cook. 'You say his name is Paul Molloy?'

'That's right. He and his wife arrived last night during dinner. They were a last-minute reservation. We had an empty cabin—the honeymoon cabin—and invited them to come. This is a week we generally reserve only for one family. They hold their family reunion here every year. But we also invited Mrs. Fletcher and another old friend from Maine, Dr. Seth Hazlitt, for the week. Turns out we might have picked a bad one for them to come.'

'You can't always control things like this,' the investigator said. 'You can't always plan for murder.'

'You're convinced it was murder?' I asked.

'Looks that way to me, Mrs. Fletcher. By the way, I'm homicide investigator Pitura, Robert Pitura.' I took his extended hand. He was even bigger than the coroner, perhaps six feet, six inches tall, with a full head of hair that came down low on his forehead, and a genuine smile.

'Pleased to meet you,' I said. 'Was it the wound to the chest that killed him?'

'Appears that way, although the doc will be the one to nail that down. You discovered the body?'

I explained the circumstances that had led Crystal to finding the body of Paul Molloy.

'See anything unusual this morning or last night, Mrs. Fletcher?'

'No. Did you get a sense of time of death?'

'The doc will determine that. The blood was crusted, though. Happened quite a while before you found him.'

'I thought the same thing.'

Pitura smiled. 'I imagine you've done some studying of murder for your books.'

'Yes, I have, a necessity for a crime novelist. I was with the deceased's wife this morning. She's at the house with Mrs. Cook.'

'She say anything interesting?'

'Interesting?'

'About her husband, where he was, why he was out here?'

'No.'

'Where was she all night?'

'In bed, I think. I woke her this morning.'

'After your ride?'

'Yes, after the body was discovered.'

'Late sleeper.'

'Evidently.'

'I'd like to speak with everyone at the ranch. They all here, Jim?'

Jim replied, 'I suppose so. All the guests, certainly. The staff. I don't think anyone's gone into town. No, sure of it. By the way, I noticed those tire tracks on the road.'

Pitura examined them, said something to a deputy, then turned to Jim and said, 'Well, might as well get to it. Sheriff Murdie will be out later. Had another scene to go to.'

We stood together as the emergency medical team brought Paul Molloy's lifeless body to the road on a gurney and slid it into the ambulance. Investigator Pitura conferred with the uniformed officers, dismissed one of them, and told the other two to stay with him.

As we approached the house, the Morrison family stood together by the pool, taking in our activities. They were all there, except for Willy. He'd probably taken to his cabin to try to calm down.

Evelyn Morrison broke from the group and came to where we'd stopped in front of the office. Jim introduced her to Investigator Pitura.

'This is extremely distressing,' she said to Jim calmly. She'd changed into a tan shirt, blue blouse, and yellow sweater, all undoubtedly bearing designer labels. 'We certainly didn't anticipate something like *this!*'

'Neither did we, Mrs. Morrison,' Jim said, keeping his tone pleasant.

'I'd like to discuss this with you further.'

'Happy to, Mrs. Morrison. But right now, I think there are more important things going on.'

She glared at him.

He smiled.

Investigator Pitura said to her, 'I'd appreciate it if you and your family remain here at the ranch and be available for questioning, Mrs. Morrison.'

'*Questioning?* Why would you want to question *us?*'

Pitura grinned and said, 'Just part of my job, ma'am. I'll try not to make it too painful.'

## CHAPTER SIX

Investigator Pitura instructed the uniformed officers to resume their examination of the area where Molloy's body had been found, and to go through the honeymoon cabin in search of anything that might shed light on his activities leading up to his death. We gathered in the Cooks' living room—Pitura, Seth, Jim and Bonnie Cook, and Geraldine Molloy.

The Gunnison County homicide investigator was as gentle as he was large. He offered comforting words to Mrs. Molloy. Once he'd established that he was a sympathetic participant, he eased into his questioning, an open notebook on his lap.

'When was the last time you saw your husband?' he asked.

She sighed, rolled her eyes as though to summon an accurate recollection, then looked at him and said, 'Last night.'

'About what time?'

'Ten. No, closer to eleven.'

'In your cabin?'

'Yes.'

'Did you both go to bed at eleven?'

'I think so. I went first, I think. Yes, I'm certain I did.'

'And what did he do?'

'Stayed up to read.'

'A book?'

'I don't know. A magazine, maybe.'

'Know the name of it?'

'No.'

'Were you awake when he came to bed?'

'I don't remember. I took a pill. I'd had trouble sleeping lately. I don't think I was awake when Paul came to bed.'

'So you're not sure he ever did come to bed.'

'I guess not.'

'What was his state of mind last night, Mrs. Molloy?'

'State of mind?'

'Yes. Was he depressed, agitated, angry about something?'

'No.'

'Had he been down about anything lately?'

'Not especially.'

'What business was he in?'

'Land development.'

Pitura smiled and shook his head. 'Afraid you'll have to be more specific than that, Mrs. Molloy. What does a land developer do?'

'Develop land. I don't mean to be evasive, but I've never been sure what Paul did. I didn't pay much attention to his business.'

'He have his own company?'

'Yes. Back home, in Nevada.'

'Las Vegas?'

'Just outside.'

'I see. What brought you to Powderhorn Ranch?'

'Paul wanted to get away for a week. I suggested Hawaii or the Caribbean. But he said he just wanted to get in the car and drive, see some of the country. A friend had been here a few years ago and suggested we spend a week. At least that's what Paul told me. He said he had trouble getting a reservation because there was a family that had booked the ranch for some sort of reunion, but that he managed to convince the owners to take us.'

'That the way it was?' Pitura asked Jim Cook.

'That's the way it was,' Jim said. 'Mr. Molloy really wanted to be here this week, said it was the only week he had. We had one empty cabin and invited them to join us.'

'How did he seem to you when he checked in?'

Jim shrugged. 'Fine, I guess. A quiet fella. Didn't have much to say at dinner.'

'What about breakfast?'

'Didn't make it for breakfast.'

'You slept in, Mrs. Molloy?'

'Yes. The pill I took was potent. I never woke up until Mrs. Fletcher came to the cabin.'

'Mind if I see the pill bottle?'

'I . . . I don't have one. I carry medications in a plastic container—vitamins, things like that. I only had one sleeping pill with me.'

'I suppose your pharmacist can tell us what sort of pill it was.'

'I'm sure he can. But why is this of interest to you? My husband was killed by some deranged person. What does it have to do with my sleeping pill?'

'Probably nothing,' Pitura said pleasantly. 'If I have any other questions, we can get together again.'

'I intend to go home,' Geraldine said.

'I'm afraid you'll have to postpone that for a few days, Mrs. Molloy.'

'But I'll have to make funeral arrangements.'

'Your husband won't be released until the autopsy has been completed,' Pitura said. 'Could be three or four days, maybe longer. In the meantime, everyone at the ranch, guests and staff alike, will have to stay for questioning.'

Geraldine stood. 'This is outrageous!'

'Mrs. Molloy, it appears that someone murdered your husband. It happened right here on the Powderhorn Ranch. I understand your wanting to get back home, but until my investigation is completed, that just won't be possible. You have children?'

'A daughter, in San Francisco.'

'Maybe she can come and be with you,' Bonnie offered. 'She can stay with us in the house.'

'My daughter and I haven't spoken in years.'

After a moment of silence, Jim Cook put his arm around Mrs. Molloy and said in his low, calm voice, 'It won't be long, Mrs. Molloy, before Mr. Pitura will have this all wrapped up and you can get back home. In the meantime, Bonnie and I will do everything we can to make it easier on you, serve meals in your cabin if you'd like, get you anything you need from town.' He turned to Pitura. 'Speaking of

66

that, Bob, I have to send one of the boys into Gunnison to pick up another guest. Her plane's due in an hour.'

'Another guest?' I said.

'Mr. Craig Morrison's wife. Couldn't come in with the rest of the family. It okay with you, Bob, if I send somebody to pick her up?'

'I suppose so, but let me talk to who you decide to send before he goes.'

'Fair enough. I'll send Jon. He should be down at the garage, fixing one of the Jeeps.'

'I'll talk to him there,' Pitura said. 'Sorry for your loss, Mrs. Molloy. You take care.'

'I'd like to lie down,' Geraldine said. 'I don't feel well.'

'Of course,' Bonnie said.

'I'll be happy to walk Mrs. Molloy to her cabin,' Seth said.

'Thank you,' Bonnie said. 'We'll check in on you later, see if you feel like some lunch.'

Seth and Mrs. Molloy were almost out the door when Pitura said, 'Mrs. Molloy, one last question before you go.'

'Yes?'

'I understand you had a handgun with you this morning.' I hadn't mentioned it to the investigator, but Seth or Jim must have.

'That's right,' she said.

'Belong to you?'

'It belonged to my husband.'

'Was it registered?'

'I don't know. He'd been attacked a year or

so ago and bought the gun for protection. I assume it was registered.'

'We can check. Naturally, we'll hold it until this is resolved. If it was properly registered, you can have it back.'

'I don't care about getting it back. When I heard someone in the cabin, I grabbed it. I didn't know who it was.'

'Perfectly understandable,' Pitura said. 'Thank you.'

When they were gone, Bonnie and I went to the kitchen, where she made a pot of tea.

'I feel terrible about this,' she said.

'Hardly calculated to make anyone feel good,' I said.

'That poor man, Mr. Molloy, and his wife.'

'I suppose it gives credence to that old saying, "Life is what happens when you're making other plans."'

'It certainly does. I feel bad for everyone, Jess, including you. Jim and I finally get you to visit, and someone is murdered. Hardly a respite from the murders you write about.'

'That's the least of it, Bonnie. As upsetting as this is, I agree with you and Jim that we should all try to make the best of it, have things go along as normally as possible. I'm sure you're right, that whoever did this has nothing whatsoever to do with the ranch.'

'I pray that's true.'

Seth returned.

'How is she?' I asked.

'Drained. Thanked me for walking her back and said she was going to bed. Best place for her.'

'There's nothing scheduled for the rest of the day,' Bonnie said, 'except lunch at twelve-thirty. There's a two-thirty ride for anyone who's interested, and we show a movie after dinner. Jim's always happy to take guests on a Jeep ride up into the mountains. But I suppose everything's subject to change, depending upon what Investigator Pitura and his people decide.'

'I'm sure he'll try to accommodate everyone, Bonnie. I'll be back in my cabin if you need anything. And please, don't hesitate to ask.'

'That goes for me, too,' Seth said.

'You're both very good friends, and very understanding. Thanks—for everything.'


## CHAPTER SEVEN

Seth and I decided that to deliberately not go to lunch as a symbolic reaction to what had happened didn't make sense. We wanted to support Jim and Bonnie's desire to keep things going as normally as possible. Besides, we were hungry.

Evidently, most of the others didn't share our view. We were joined only by Chris and

Marisa Morrison, Evelyn's brother, Robert, and a handful of staff. Joel served a taco salad with bowls of chopped onions, sour cream, and salsa, peaches with cream cheese, and chocolate chip brownies for dessert.

'The rest of your family skipping lunch?' Seth asked Chris.

'They said they weren't hungry. Can't blame them, I guess, considering what's happened.'

'I was interviewed by the police,' wrangler Andy Wilson said. 'Jon was, too, before he went to town to pick up Mrs. Morrison.'

'What did they ask you?' Sue, one of the cabin girls, said.

'Where I was last night and this morning.'

'What did you tell them?'

'Where I was. I did my laundry last night before we got together to watch TV. Remember?'

'I didn't see you in the laundry room,' Sue said. 'I did my laundry last night, too.'

'I must have been there before you,' Andy replied, a tinge of anger to his voice.

'The investigator—what's his name? Pitura? —wants to interview us this afternoon,' Chris Morrison said.

'Why they would interview us is beyond me,' said his wife, Marisa. She guffawed. 'Surely, he doesn't suspect anyone from this family.'

'They have to do their job,' Seth said. 'They can't rule anyone out when a murder's been committed.' He took another helping of taco

70

salad.

'Jon said he saw a stranger on the road early this morning,' Andy said.

'That's interesting,' I said. 'Did he tell the investigator?'

'I guess so. He interviewed us separately.'

'Has any of your family seen anything unusual?' I asked Chris. 'I saw that some of you were up early this morning.'

'Not that anybody said. How about you, Mrs. Fletcher? I saw you walking early.'

'Yes, I was, but I saw nothing out of the ordinary.'

'You'll probably solve this before the cops,' Chris said, laughing. 'I mean, with all the murder mysteries you've written, you probably already have a theory. Am I right?'

'No, you are wrong, Mr. Morrison. I haven't a clue.'

'What about his wife?' Marisa asked. 'She's a strange-o.'

'She's very upset, as can be imagined. She doesn't know when he left their cabin.'

'How can that be?' Chris asked. 'You know what they say about murder.'

'What do they say, Mr. Morrison?' Seth asked.

'*Cherchez la femme.*'

'What does that mean?' Sue, the cabin girl, asked.

'It means "Look for the woman in the case,"' I said. 'Alexandre Dumas.'

71

Hand on hip, Sue asked, 'Why the woman?'

'Most murders are crimes of passion,' Chris Morrison responded. 'You always look to the spouse first. Isn't that right, Mrs. Fletcher?'

'I suppose so,' I said.

'If you ask me, his wife did him in,' Chris said. 'They didn't look all that happy at dinner last night.'

'Ready, Seth?' I asked, standing.

Robert Morrison, Evelyn's brother, hadn't said anything during lunch. As Seth and I stepped outside, he followed.

'A word, Mrs. Fletcher?'

'Yes?'

Morrison looked at Seth.

'Think I'll stroll up and see if Mrs. Molloy is awake,' Seth said, 'and ask if she needs anything.'

'That would be nice, Seth. Let me know if I can help.'

'*Ayuh.*'

Morrison and I walked to the end of the main lodge and turned the corner, stopping at a large outdoor sink where lucky fishermen cleaned their catch. It had clouded over since we went to lunch, and turned chilly.

'I understand you're good friends with Mr. and Mrs. Cook, Mrs. Fletcher.'

'That's right. We were neighbors in Maine.'

'I'm sure you can understand that my sister and I are extremely upset over what's happened.'

72

'As we all are.'

'Perhaps not. You and your physician friend are here as guests of the Cooks. A relaxing, carefree week. We, on the other hand, are here not only to allow family members to get together socially, but to iron out some family business.'

'Oh? What sort of business?'

'Succession issues, corporate structure—we always use this week as a retreat of sorts, a chance to get away from the pressures of the boardroom and discuss things in a peaceful atmosphere. The point I wish to make, Mrs. Fletcher, is that to be intruded upon by this investigation will hamper our ability to resolve certain business issues.'

'It will be an intrusion into all our lives,' I said, not pleased at the direction the conversation was taking. Obviously, he felt he and his wealthy family were above being investigated.

'Let me get to the point,' he said. His voice was flat, a monotone, and grating. 'Mr. and Mrs. Cook obviously are well known in this area. I noticed that the homicide investigator—Pitura, is it?—is on a first name basis with them. They call him by his first name, too. Surely, they could make a case with him that no member of my family could possibly be involved in this sordid mess. He could also prevail, using the health of his business as a basis. We're very good customers of this ranch, Mrs. Fletcher. We come here every year and are generous with our treatment of the staff. I really think that—'

'Are you suggesting I intervene with the Cooks, Mr. Morrison, and ask them to seek some sort of special treatment for you and your family?'

'That would be very much appreciated.'

'I'm afraid I'll have to disappoint you. There's been a brutal murder committed on the ranch. Everyone must be considered a suspect until the police solve the case. I understand how painful this is for your family, but—'

'I thought you might be more co-operative, Mrs. Fletcher.'

'I *am* co-operative, Mr. Morrison, but at the moment, my co-operation is extended to Investigator Pitura and his people. Excuse me. I want to check on Mrs. Molloy—the widow.'

The Morrison gene, the one that seemed to imbue each family member with a sourness, came through on his face. I started to leave, stopped, turned, and asked, 'Mr. Morrison, what business is your family in?'

He answered by walking in the direction of the cabins.

Seth was coming from the honeymoon cabin as I approached.

'How is she?' I asked.

'Still resting. I spoke with her for a few minutes. I think the shock has set in. Always

74

takes a while for that to happen. Any plans for the rest of the afternoon?'

'No. I considered asking Jim to take me on a Jeep ride, but I'm sure he won't be free to do that for a day or two, until the investigation winds down.'

'Sounds unduly optimistic,' Seth said. 'Probably will be going on all week and beyond.'

'Cup of tea?'

'Don't mind if I do.'

I made tea in my cabin, and we sat on the porch, watching the comings and goings of Investigator Pitura and the other officers. The main lodge had been established as the center for interviews. Members of the Morrison family entered individually, each emerging a half hour later while another person waited to go in.

'Wonder when the investigator will get around to us,' Seth said.

'Soon enough, I'm sure. Have you heard anything about the weapon?'

'No.'

'Once they determine what sort of weapon was used, it might help narrow the inquiry.'

'*If* they find it. Hardly likely.'

'You never know.'

We lingered for a half hour until I announced I might put in an hour's fishing on Cebolla Creek.

'Feelin' up to it, Jessica?'

'It would take my mind off things like

murder. The world—the *real* world—always disappears when I'm on a stream. Care to join me?'

'You know I don't fish, at least not anymore.'

'Good chance to take it up again.'

'No, you go on. I think I'll do some reading back at my cabin.'

Fly fishing takes preparation. I went inside and slipped into lightweight stockingfoot waders, which came up to my chest and were secured over my shoulders with suspenders. Next came protective wading socks, after which I put on my wading boots and laced them up. That portion of the ritual completed, I donned my wading vest with its multiple pockets, attached a small net to a ring at the back of the vest with an elastic cord, put together my fourpiece Hardy rod and reel, chose a small dry fly that had been tied to emulate natural insect life on a stream, put on my peaked fishing hat, and left the cabin. Already, the tragic event of the morning was fading from consciousness.

Jim Cook saw me heading for the creek. He'd just come from the lodge, accompanied by Investigator Pitura, who patted him on the back and walked to the house. Jim caught up with me.

'Glad to see you're taking it in stride, Jess,' he said, 'going on with some sort of normal activity.'

'I think it's important to do that,' I said.

'Absolutely.'

'How are the interviews going?'

'Pretty well, I guess. Bob Pitura has a nice way of getting people to open up.'

'Yes. I noticed that when he was questioning Mrs. Molloy. Have you been present at any of the interviews?'

'Yes, I have. Surprised that Bob would allow that. But he said he thought having either Bonnie or me there would put some of the staff at ease.' He laughed ruefully. 'Questioning the staff must be just routine for Bob. I'm sure he knows nobody working at this ranch could possibly have murdered anyone.'

I didn't voice my thought of the moment. It was natural for Jim to feel that way, just as the Morrison family found it inconceivable that any of its members would be viewed with suspicion. I suppose I felt the same about Seth and me.

But *somebody* had killed Paul Molloy. Someone had stabbed or shot him in the chest.

'Any word on the weapon?' I asked.

'No. I spoke with Sheriff Murdie a little while ago. He said he'd be here late afternoon. He's tied up with another investigation.'

'Is there much crime out here?' I asked.

'Hardly any. Not murder, anyway. I think there's been two since we bought the Powderhorn. They recently solved one going back seventeen years. A young girl was killed

77

then. The murderer was doing twenty years in Tennessee for armed robbery. Amazing, huh, how they could come up with the killer after all those years?'

'It certainly is. Your Sheriff Murdie and his people must be pretty good at what they do.'

'I guess they are. The sheriff's a nice sorta fella. I think you'll enjoy meeting him. Well, I'll let you get on to your fishing. If you don't have any luck, there's always the stocked pond.'

'I hope I won't have to resort to that. Too much like shooting fish in a barrel. See you later, Jim.'

Cebolla Creek is fast-moving and not difficult to access from the bank, at least the portion immediately on ranch property. It's a narrow stream with a lot of overhanging branches, making casting difficult. A section of it beyond the stables and corrals is considerably wider, but I decided to save that for another day. Working on the narrow portion would allow me to practice what's called a roll-cast, in which the rod isn't brought up behind. Instead, you leave the tip down near the water and 'whip' the line out into the current.

I found a spot with relatively secure footing and went to work, laying the tiny fly where I wanted it and watching it drift with the current until it was time to cast again. I'd been at it for forty-five minutes, during which time the sun disappeared, the skies blackened, rain fell, and then the sun shone brightly again.

I snagged the fly on a piece of deadwood. I tried to yank it free, but the fly broke away from the tippet, the hair-thin filament at the end of the line. I chose a similar fly from a box in one of my vest's pockets, tied it on the tippet, and cast. It hadn't traveled more than six feet when a trout broke the water's surface and went for it. I yanked back on the line. I had it. My heart tripped as it always does when I've managed to fool a fish into thinking my offering at the end of the line is the real thing. But I knew I had to play it with care. I remove the barbs from all my hooks, which makes releasing a fish considerably easier on me, and on the fish, but that more easily slips from the mouth when bringing a fish in.

Here was where skill was paramount. I made sure my feet were solid and began to haul in line, slowly, keeping it taut to maintain a constant pressure. The fish leaped from the water, then disappeared beneath it. I continued to play it, wanting to net it before it fought too long and exhausted itself.

I now had it close and reached around to bring the net forward with my right hand, while holding the rod in my left. 'Easy now,' I said aloud. 'Just another few feet and—'

The noise was sudden and startling. There was someone in the bushes behind me. I turned. In doing so, I allowed the line to

79

slacken. The fish slipped the hook and was gone. So was I. My right foot went out from under me. As hard as I tried to maintain my balance, I couldn't, and tumbled into the water, valiantly attempting to hold on to the rod. Water poured into my waders; I'd neglected to wear a belt around my waist to prevent that from happening. As I fell, I managed to see what had caused the noise—a person. I couldn't make out who it was; he or she pushed through the bushes and was gone from my sight.

Fortunately, the water at that point in the Cebolla isn't deep, and I had no fear of being pulled under by my waders, which were now like water-filled balloons. A surprising number of fly fishermen die each year in just such accidents. I almost did a few years ago in Scotland.

I dragged myself over rocks to the bank, where I sprawled and caught my breath. My mishap had turned into nothing more than an embarrassment, and the loss of a fish, which I would have let go anyway. I raised my legs to allow some of the water to drain from my waders. Now able to maneuver, I climbed the bank to where the bushes lined the Cebolla. I put my hand to my head. My hat was gone, my favorite fishing hat. Better that than all of me, I decided.

I started in the direction of my cabin, looking down as I did. Two footprints were directly in front of me. They appeared to be fresh. I bent over and touched the indentation one had made in the earth. It was pointed away from the creek, toward the cabins. Same with the second print.

As I headed for my cabin—waddled is more accurate—Bonnie Cook was crossing the grassy strip. 'What happened to you?' she asked, eyes wide.

'Slipped in the stream. No damage except for a lost favorite fishing hat.'

'Those rocks in there can be slippery.'

'I know. I was startled by—'

'By what?'

'Must have been a bird, or one of the dogs. Anyway, Bonnie, I caught a trout and almost netted it.'

'You fishing fanatics always amaze me. Nothing fazes you as long as you catch a fish.'

'I'd better get out of these wet clothes,' I said, 'before I catch cold.'

'Yes, you'd better.'

'How's things going with the investigation?'

'All right, I guess. Bob Pitura is staying for dinner. So is Sheriff Murdie. They'd like to talk to us as a group.'

'Okay. See you then.'

I changed into a running suit and sneakers, grabbed a small point-and-shoot camera and cloth measuring tape from my bag, left the cabin, and returned to where I'd seen the footprints. I knelt and examined them closely.

They'd obviously been made by a man's shoe or boot—or a woman wearing such a shoe. I snapped a picture of each print, then measured them, aware that what I came up with could be considered only approximate. They measured size eleven.

There certainly was nothing wrong with someone standing on the bank of the Cebolla and watching me fish. People do it all the time. But why would he, or she, have bolted the minute I turned around? If I'd seen someone slip and fall in the water, my immediate reaction would have been to offer to help, not run. My assumption had to be that whoever it was didn't want me to know that he, or she, had been observing me.

As I stood there pondering, homicide investigator Pitura came up behind.

'Looking for clues?' he asked pleasantly, and with a broad smile.

'No. I was just—'

He bent over and looked closely at one of the footprints. 'Is this what piqued your interest, Mrs. Fletcher?'

'Yes. Actually, I—'

'Think they belong to Mr. Molloy's killer?'

'No.' I explained what had happened.

'I agree with you,' he said. 'Why would someone not want you to know he was watching you?'

'Terminal shyness,' I offered, tongue in cheek.

'Hmmm.'

'I understand you and the sheriff want to speak with us as a group at dinner.'

'That's right. I think everyone at the ranch deserves to be kept abreast of what we've done, and what we'll be doing.'

'An unusual approach for someone investigating a murder.'

'How so?'

'Keeping suspects informed of the investigation's progress.'

He smiled. 'Maybe I'm taking a page from one of your murder mysteries, Mrs. Fletcher. I've read most of them. Many feature unusual investigative techniques. I understand you've solved your share of real murders.'

'Wrong place, wrong time, I'm afraid.'

'Well, this looks like another case of that. Mind if I pick your brain as we go forward?'

'Of course not.'

'I'll have plaster casts made of those prints.'

'If you wish.'

'I wish. See you at dinner.'

## CHAPTER EIGHT

Sue, the cabin girl, had carried the evening's fare—fried chicken, 'melt in your mouth' potatoes, broccoli casserole, homemade biscuits, and apple pie—to Geraldine Molloy in the honeymoon cabin. Whether the grieving widow would be up for such a large dinner was conjecture. Bonnie had suggested to Mrs. Molloy that she might feel better if she was with people, but Geraldine declined the advice. 'I need to be by myself,' she'd said. Which, of course, we all understood.

There was a sense of heightened anticipation in the main lodge when we gathered for dinner. The main room was large enough for factions to congregate in opposite corners. The Morrison family had grown; Craig's wife, Veronica, had arrived in late afternoon, driven in the Cooks' suburban by wrangler Jon Adler. I'd watched as she was greeted by Jim, his omnipresent video camera rolling as she stepped from the vehicle. She was a stunning woman, approximately forty years old, tall and full-figured—buxom would be an appropriate word—her features fine, long blond hair allowed to fall naturally over her shoulders. No one had bothered to introduce her, so I went to where she sat and extended my hand.

'The young man who drove me from the airport said the famous murder mystery, writer, Jessica Fletcher, was here,' she said.

'Unfortunately, there's been a *real* murder,' I said. 'But I'm sure you already know that.'

'Yes, Craig told me.'

'Did you just fly into Gunnison this afternoon?'

'Yes.'

'Smooth flight?'

'Yes. Smooth as silk, as they say. Nice to meet you, Mrs. Fletcher. I hope we can find some time to talk while we're here.'

I rejoined Seth at the games table. 'This Mrs. Morrison seems more pleasant and gracious than the others,' I said into his ear.

'That's nice to hear,' he said.

Sheriff Murdie and his homicide investigator, Bob Pitura, sat next to each other near the entrance to the dining room and spoke to each other in hushed tones. Jim and Bonnie were in and out as they juggled preparing for dinner and being host and hostess to their guests. Unlike the previous evening, the staff did not mingle with us before dinner. It was as though sides had been chosen and we were preparing for competition, maybe a game of charades, or statues.

Jim eventually appeared in the doorway and, with his customary wide smile, announced that dinner was ready. We filed into the dining room and took what had become our usual seats at the long table. I was glad to see that some of the wranglers joined us. Their presence tended to perk up spirits. The only guest missing was Craig Morrison's teen daughter, Pauline. I asked about her.

'This episode has upset her terribly,' Evelyn Morrison said. 'She's been in tears all day.'

'Sheriff Murdie will be saying a few words,'

Jim said as he started passing platters. 'Any time it suits you, Richard.'

The sheriff was six feet tall, solidly built, close-cropped black hair with a touch of gray at the temples, and a neatly trimmed mustache. He wore glasses. He was dressed in a striped sport shirt and jeans.

'Maybe your guests would rather eat first, Jim.'

'Up to them.'

'*I* have some questions I'd like answered,' Evelyn Morrison said sternly.

Murdie smiled. 'I'll answer anything I can, Mrs. Morrison, although there will be some areas I'll have to avoid.'

'Why are we being questioned?' Evelyn asked.

'You mean you and your family?'

'Yes. We're guests at this ranch for the week. We've been coming here for years. We not only use this week each year to bond together, we use it as a retreat at which to discuss sensitive, important business.'

Murdie listened attentively, helping himself to chicken as the platter reached him.

Evelyn's brother, Robert, added, 'Your interrogation of us represents an unnecessary intrusion, Sheriff. It's obvious that the murder—if it *was* murder—was committed by some outsider, some nut passing by.'

A pleasant, concerned expression never left the sheriff's face. He asked, 'Why do you think it might not have been murder, Mr. Morrison?'

'It could have been an accident. One look at Molloy and it was obvious to me he drank a lot.'

'Oh?' said Murdie. 'What in his appearance led you to that conclusion?'

'It was written all over his face.'

'An Irish face,' Murdie said, buttering a biscuit, the subtle accusation that Morrison was dealing in stereotypes not lost on me.

'Maybe we ought to see what the sheriff and Mr. Pitura have come up with before we get into why he has to question us—*all* of us,' Bonnie said.

'Good idea,' Seth said. 'Any progress, Sheriff?'

Murdie turned to Pitura. 'Why don't you fill these good folks in on the investigation, Bob.'

Pitura said, 'Not too much to report.' He turned to Robert Morrison. 'It *was* murder, Mr. Morrison. Mr. Molloy was stabbed in the chest by some sort of weapon. I spoke to the ME before dinner. It wasn't a sharp knife. It was thick and rough, based upon his initial examination of the wound.'

'Seems to me finding such a weapon shouldn't be difficult,' Chris Morrison said. 'The killer probably dropped it in the woods. Right, Mrs. Fletcher?'

I said nothing.

'We've searched the woods,' Pitura said.

'Naturally, I'm sorry you've had to take some time from your week at the Powderhorn to be questioned. I've tried to keep the intrusion to a minimum, and will continue to do so as the week progresses.'

'There's to be more?' Evelyn asked.

'Oh, yes,' said Pitura. 'Our questioning of you has only been preliminary. But again, I'll try to—'

'This is outrageous,' Robert Morrison said.

'Perhaps we should simply pack up and go home,' said Evelyn.

'I'm afraid that won't be possible, at least for a few days,' Sheriff Murdie said.

'I beg to differ with you, Sheriff,' Robert Morrison said. 'I'm an attorney. You have no legal right to detain us here.'

'Well, I'm not a lawyer, Mr. Morrison, but I do know that I have the legal authority to do exactly that; detain you until I'm satisfied we've completed our questioning of each of you. Of course, no one's going to stand guard to make sure you don't leave. But if you do decide to take off, I'll just have to dispatch some of my people to Denver and continue questioning you in conjunction with your local authorities. But do you know what?'

'What?'

'It seems to me that if you and your family had absolutely nothing to do with this—and, I hasten to add I'm sure that's the case—it seems to me you'd want to stay and be as helpful as possible. It seems to me that anyone who can't deal with being questioned might—and I emphasize *might*—have some reason for it.'

I covered my smile with my hand. This sheriff of Gunnison County, Colorado, knew exactly how to deal with people like the Morrisons.

'I asked Mrs. Fletcher if she had any leads,' Chris Morrison said. 'She said she didn't, but I don't believe her.'

Homicide Investigator Pitura looked at me and said, 'I've already suggested I might pick Mrs. Fletcher's sizable brain, considering her track record in solving murders.'

The sheriff said, 'Good idea. Well, Mrs. Fletcher, *do* you have any leads, any good ideas about who might have done this?'

'None whatsoever,' I said.

Chris said, 'Come on, Mrs. Fletcher. Tell us who done the dastardly deed, and we can all forget about it and enjoy the rest of the week.' He was beginning to annoy me.

'Jessica Fletcher *writes* about murder,' Seth said. 'She doesn't involve herself personally.'

'Ready for pie?' Jim Cook asked. He asked it of Willy, the nervous Morrison cousin who'd been with us on the ride when Paul Molloy's body was discovered. He responded by pushing back his chair and saying, 'Excuse me. I have a headache.'

When he was gone, Sheriff Murdie said,

'Taking this pretty hard, I see.'

'Willy is high-strung,' Evelyn said. 'Being questioned by the police puts a terrible strain on him. I hope you won't put any credence in what he might tell you.'

I glanced at the sheriff and his homicide investigator and could almost see their minds working. Evelyn's comment said something quite apart from what she might have intended, and I was certain the police would now make it a point to spend more time with Cousin Willy.

As the staff cleared the table, Jim asked, 'Have you decided on a movie?'

'I'd forgotten about that,' I said.

'Got some fine old Tom Mix and Gene Autry flicks. Plenty of John Wayne, too.'

'I'd enjoy seeing a good old-fashioned western shoot-em-up,' I said. 'Seth?'

'Don't mind if I do.'

'I'll make popcorn,' Jim said. 'Go pick a film, and I'll rack it up.' He turned to Sheriff Murdie and Investigator Pitura. 'You fellas want to stay?'

'No,' Murdie said. 'We have to get back to town. I'm leaving a uniformed officer on the premises. He'll be in his car at the main entrance to the ranch. Naturally, no one is to go near the crime scene. Bob will be back first thing in the morning to continue the investigation. Good night, everybody. A pleasure to share a meal with you. The chicken was especially good, Bonnie.'

'Thank you, Sheriff. Safe home. Come in time for breakfast, Bob.'

I was surprised that most of the Morrisons stayed for the movie. I wondered whether they did so to show that they were not intimidated or deterred by something as mundane as murder. Perhaps that was being unduly cynical. Maybe they simply loved western movies.

Since no one seemed especially interested in selecting a film, Seth did the honors, choosing one of director John Ford's greatest, *My Darling Clementine,* a 1946 black-and-white classic starring Henry Fonda as Marshal Wyatt Earp and Victor Mature as Doc Holliday. Jim handed us bowls of popcorn, inserted the video in the VCR, dimmed the lights, and we settled back for a night at the movies.

But as engrossing as the story was, my mind kept wandering to everything that had happened since our arrival at the Powderhorn Ranch. Foremost in my thoughts was the weapon used to kill Paul Molloy. Either the murderer had taken it with him, or had ditched it somewhere in the vicinity. Cebolla Creek, or the stocked fishing pond, would be the most logical of places, and I made a mental note to suggest to Bob Pitura in the morning that they be dragged. I also wondered whether the cabins had been searched. Mine certainly hadn't been, at least not to my knowledge. Pitura had said the weapon was rough, unlike a knife. What could it be, then? Some sort of poker? A screwdriver? Whatever it was had certainly done the job.

I also thought during the movie of someone having observed me while fishing that afternoon. Pitura said he would have plaster casts made of the footprints, but to what end? Whoever it was behind the bushes hadn't done anything nefarious. But why hadn't that person stayed when I turned at the sound he or she had made? Why the need to crash through the bushes to escape being seen by me?

I'd taken note of shoes worn by people at dinner, an unproductive exercise. The prints in the dirt had measured size eleven—maybe eleven and a half. There didn't seem to be any distinguishing marks left by the soles. An unusually small or large print would have helped narrow it down.

Seth dozed off during the film, not an unusual occurrence. When THE END appeared on the screen, Jim turned up the lights. I looked around. Most of the Morrison family had left. Only Chris, the younger brother, and Craig's wife, Veronica, remained.

'Enjoy it?' I asked.

'Henry Fonda has always been one of my favorites,' Veronica said.

'Mine, too,' I said.

'I don't like westerns,' Chris said.

'They're just stories with a western setting,' I said.

'I think they're dumb.'

Seth yawned, stretched, and stood. 'Past my bedtime,' he said. 'Jessica?'

'I'm not sleepy. I think I'll sit here a bit.'

'As you wish. Good evening, Mr. and Mrs. Morrison.'

'Good evening, Doctor. Sleep well.'

Jim excused himself. So did Chris Morrison. Veronica crossed the room and sat next to me on the couch. 'I understand you discovered the body,' she said.

'No. One of the wranglers did. I was riding with the group she led.'

'Did you actually see the body?'

'Yes.'

'How dreadful. They say he was stabbed in the chest.'

'So it seems, although a final determination of cause of death hasn't been made yet.'

'Did you know Mr.—? His name escapes me.'

'Molloy. Paul Molloy. He and his wife had dinner with us last night. A nice couple. Quiet.'

'Here one moment having a pleasant dinner, dead the next.' She wrapped her arms about herself and shuddered.

'Makes you appreciate each day you're alive,' I said.

'It certainly does. Chris says the local police are probably a bunch of bunglers and will never solve it.'

'That's not my impression of them,' I said. 'They seem quite astute and professional.'

'I hope you're right. Well, I suppose I'd better get back to the cabin. Oh, Craig tells me you're a pilot.'

'A fledgling one.'

'I fly, too. I got my license a year ago.'

'How wonderful. Do you get a chance to fly much?'

'Not as much as I'd like. Good night, Mrs. Fletcher.'

'Good night. And it's Jessica.'

She gave me her hand. 'And I'm Veronica.'

I watched her walk from the room. She was a stunning woman who might easily have been a model. I recalled Evelyn's harsh words to Craig about her and wondered if it could involve jealousy—two beautiful, proud women vying for attention within a family.

I stood outside and looked up into a pristine sky, then peered down the road to where a marked police car was parked. Funny, how even something as vile as murder can be forgotten when other things intervene, like a movie, or a good meal.

*Murder!*

For the first time since the morning I was overcome with the grim reality that someone had been brutally killed, and whoever did it was still at large.

I willed all my senses into an alert status and quickly crossed the grass to my cabin. I'm not

94

by nature a fearful person, and have always been successful at preventing my mind from playing games with me. But as soon as I was inside, I checked the closets and behind the bathroom shower curtain, then locked the front door.

The killings in the movie had been only make-believe.

This was real life.

## CHAPTER NINE

'Everyone sleep well?' Jim Cook asked as we gathered for bacon and eggs, and peach coffee cake for dessert. Sheriff Murdie hadn't come to the ranch that morning, but Bob Pitura was there at breakfast.

Noncommittal murmurs came from around the table. I said nothing; I hadn't slept well, waking frequently to sounds, real and imagined. But Seth looked refreshed and alert, even jovial.

'The sign-up sheet for today's supper ride is posted outside the lodge,' Bonnie announced. 'Will everybody be joining us? It's a beautiful ride, and Jim does a great cookout.'

Cousin Willy squirmed in his chair and winced.

'We'll use the Jeeps for anybody who doesn't want to ride,' Jim said.

95

'We will *all* *r*ide,' Evelyn proclaimed. 'This is, after all, a ranch.'

'Good to hear,' Jim said. 'Got to keep the horses working. Did you hear about the church that hired one of its out-of-work parishioners to paint the church?'

'No,' Seth and I said. 'Tell us about the fellow who painted the church.'

Jim laughed and continued: 'This fella decided to thin the paint so he'd make a bigger profit. He kept thinning and thinning. Finally, he was at the top of the steeple when light lit up the sky. There was a clap of thunder, and a loud voice came from the heavens. ' "Repaint, repaint, but thin no more!" '

'Oh, Jim,' Bonnie said, shaking her head.

We all laughed, except Evelyn, who said to Bob Pitura, 'I suppose we'll be subjected to more questioning today.'

'Yes, ma'am,' Pitura said, 'but I'll try to not interfere with the day's activities.'

'As though that were possible,' Evelyn said, pushing away from the table, standing, and leading her family from the lodge, like a mother duck being trailed by recent hatchlings. Seth and I joined Jim beneath the overhang at the front of the lodge.

'Going on the morning ride?' he asked.

'Not me,' Seth said. 'Still sore from yesterday. But I'll be ready to saddle up again this afternoon.'

'You, Jess?'

'I think I'll fish this morning. That trout that got away yesterday is there waiting for me. I can feel it.'

'Go get 'em,' Jim said. 'I'll pop down and capture it for posterity on videotape.'

'Just don't have the camera rolling if I fall again.'

'Bonnie told me about yesterday. Be careful. Those rocks can be slippery, even if you do have felt soles on your wading boots.'

Jim walked away as Bob Pitura joined us. 'Grab a few minutes with you, Mrs. Fletcher?'

'Of course. Is it my turn to be questioned?'

'No. There's something else I'd like to discuss with you.'

'Oh?'

'See you later, Jessica,' Seth said. 'Think I'll get back to my book.'

'I'd like you to join us, Dr. Hazlitt, if you don't mind.'

'Don't mind a bit.'

We went back inside the lodge and sat in the large main room. Sue, the cabin girl, poured fresh coffee, and placed a platter of leftover peach coffee cake in front of us.

'Before I forget it,' I said, 'I was wondering whether you intended to drag the creek for the weapon.'

'It's on the agenda, if we don't find it first. The stocked pond, too.'

'Good.'

'Before I left town this morning, I got

together with Sheriff Murdie and the medical examiner. Mr. Molloy died of that stab wound. No surprise, of course, but always nice to have things officially confirmed.'

'Did your ME establish a time of death?'

'Sometime between two and eight.'

'That's a pretty wide window,' Seth said.

'Yes, it is, but it's unlikely the murder took place during daylight hours. Gets light here about five, five-fifteen. I'd say it happened between two and five.'

'Makes sense,' I said. 'Has any of your questioning revealed anything? Or maybe that question is out of line.'

'Ordinarily, I wouldn't talk about the results of my questioning. But in your case I think I will.'

'Why? Should I be flattered?'

'Perhaps.' He grinned. 'I said I wanted to talk to you about other things, Mrs. Fletcher. With you, too, Dr. Hazlitt.'

'We're listening,' Seth said.

'I've been doing homicide investigations for more years than I'm willing to admit.'

'I didn't think there were that many homicides to investigate in Gunnison County,' I said.

'There aren't. But I go way back with Sheriff Murdie, to when we were both Marines in San Diego, and thirteen years with the Denver PD. Plenty of murders in Denver. The point is, it's been my experience that in a situation like we have here, interviewing the guests and staff probably won't produce much in the way of information, especially since there's a large family involved. Of course, you never know. Every once in a while somebody tells you something that's totally unexpected. I'll continue with my official questioning for as long as I think it's productive. My *official* questioning.'

'I take it there's to be some *unofficial* questioning.'

'I hope so. That is, if you and Dr. Hazlitt are willing.'

'Us?' Seth said.

'Yes, sir. The way I figure it, Mrs. Fletcher has the perfect reason for asking questions. She is, after all, a noted writer of crime novels, and I'm sure you're always researching crime and criminals.'

'I do a great deal of that.'

'And you, Dr. Hazlitt, being a physician and close friend, gives you your own reason for asking questions. Maybe you help Mrs. Fletcher research the medical aspects of her books.'

'I've done a little of that,' Seth said proudly.

'He certainly has,' I said, smiling at my friend.

Pitura continued. 'I just thought you might engage the others in conversation, find out more about them, where they're coming from, their views of what happened, things like that. You know, friendly chitchat, but with a purpose.'

'I see. I'm willing, of course, but I can't conceive of anyone telling me very much that would be useful.'

'Then again, Mrs. Fletcher, you might come up with something that's very useful. Willing to try?'

'Of course.'

'You, Dr. Hazlitt?'

*'Ayuh.'*

'Pardon?'

'That's Maine for yes,' I said.

'Oh. Well, I appreciate the help. By the way, we did a background check on Paul Molloy. He's from Las Vegas.'

'So he said.'

'Strange background. A little of this, a little of that. Land deals, most of them gone sour. One of those men who's always looking for the big score rather than working hard to earn a series of smaller successes. Has some shadowy government background, too.'

'Government?'

'Connected with the CIA, or so he told people. Lived in the old Soviet Union for a while. Middle East, too.'

'Hmmm. What about his wife? How long have they been married?'

'Not long.'

'Really?'

'In fact, they're not—married.'

Seth and I looked at each other. I said, 'But they introduced themselves as man and wife. And I think she said they had a daughter in San Francisco. Estranged from her, I believe.'

'There's no record of any marriage in the Nevada files. Of course, they might have been married elsewhere. But I doubt it. My sources in Las Vegas say Paul Molloy has been a bachelor for years.'

'Strange,' Seth said.

'Maybe you can start there, Mrs. Fletcher, try to get to the bottom of their relationship.'

'Then that's what I'll do.'

'And don't ignore the staff of the Powderhorn. For instance, the chef'—he consulted a small notebook—'Joel Louden. Bonnie told me he was a last-minute substitute for the chef they'd hired for the season. The original guy just picked up and left a week ago. Mr. Louden drives onto the ranch the very afternoon the chef left, has good credentials as a cook, and is hired on the spot. Bonnie and Jim had their reservations about taking on someone whom they don't know very well. They pick their staff from hundreds of applications each year, and dig deep into their backgrounds, references, things like that. But they were in a real bind. Bonnie says Louden was personable and well-mannered. Cooks good, too, she says.'

'Lucky to get him, I'd say,' said Seth.

'I suppose so. His last cooking job was in Las Vegas.'

'Where Mr. Molloy was from.'

'Right. I'll catch up with you later.' When Pitura was gone, Seth said, 'Didn't bargain for this, did we, when we decided to come to the Powderhorn Ranch?'

'No. Sorry we said we'd do it?'

'Not at all. Should provide some added adventure for you, Jessica, maybe displace any notions of flying a plane when we get back.'

'An ulterior motive.'

He grinned. 'I have them now and then. Going fishing?'

'Yes. And while I'm catching that trout again, why don't you go up and see how Mrs. Molloy—if that's who she really is—is doing. Apply some of your patented bedside manner, chat her up, as the British say.

'I believe I will. See you at lunch?'

'Yes. Clam chowder and turkey salad, I believe, prepared by a real-life Las Vegas chef.'

## CHAPTER TEN

I fished for an hour with no success, if success is defined by catching something. For me, and most fly fishers I know, just being on a fast-moving stream, surrounded by nature, is success enough.

After trying a variety of flies, I reeled in my line and slowly walked along the edge of the Cebolla in search of a deeper pool where trout might congregate, or a fallen log beneath which they often take refuge. I found neither after walking a few hundred yards, and decided to return to my cabin. I stepped up onto a relatively flat bit of land and had taken steps away from the creek when something caught my eye. I turned and looked closer. It was a long metal object lying on a patch of close-clipped grass. I crouched and examined it. Could this be the weapon used to stab Paul Molloy to death?

I straightened up and looked around. I didn't want to touch it, of course, but also didn't want to leave it unattended. But then I saw the head wrangler, Joe Walker, walking a horse from a small paddock where sick members of the herd were quarantined.

'Joe,' I shouted.

He saw me and waved.

'Could you help me with something?'

'In a minute.' He tied the horse's reins to a post and came to me. 'Hi, Mrs. Fletcher. What's up?'

'This.' I pointed to the object on the ground.

'One of the wranglers must have dropped it.'

He started to bend over to pick it up, but I stopped him. 'It might be the murder weapon,'

I said.

He recoiled.

'Do you recognize it?' I asked.

'Sure. It's a rasp. A round one.'

'With a very pointed tip.'

'Right.'

'What's it used for?'

'Filing down things, shaping wood, metal. We have a few of them at the stable.'

'You do? Would you know if one is missing?'

He shrugged. 'Probably. Jim insists we maintain a good inventory of every tool. We keep things like this in a separate wooden box.'

'Joe, would you find Investigator Pitura and ask him to come here? I'll stay with this.'

'Sure.'

They returned a few minutes later. Pitura looked at the rasp, then at me. 'It was just lying here?' he asked.

'Yes.'

'We searched this area thoroughly yesterday. Every inch.'

'I was surprised, too, to stumble across it so easily. It's sitting on a patch of grass that's considerably shorter than the grass around it.'

'It must have been put here last night or this morning.'

'Do you think—?'

'That it's the murder weapon? That's easy enough to check out with the ME.'

'Mr. Walker says they have a number of

these in the stable.'

Pitura turned to Walker. 'Would you know if one was missing?'

'Mrs. Fletcher asked me that. I said we probably would.'

'Okay.' Pitura pulled a plastic bag from his jacket and deftly slipped the rasp into it. 'I'll have one of the officers run this into town.'

'Okay if I go now?' Walker asked. 'I have to treat one of the horses. He has strangles.'

'Strangles?' I asked.

'A disease. Can be fatal if it's not treated right.'

'Sure, go ahead,' Pitura said to Walker. 'You'll be around all afternoon?'

'Yup, except when we go on the supper ride.'

'I'll catch up with you right after lunch.'

'Glad you came across this, Mrs. Fletcher,' Pitura said as we walked to the center of the ranch.

'If I hadn't,' I said, 'someone else certainly would have. Whoever put it there wanted it found, and as soon as possible.'

'I agree. Have you had a chance to follow up on my suggestion that you and the doctor talk to the Morrison family and staff?'

'I'm afraid not. I headed right for the creek. But Dr. Hazlitt was going to see if he could speak with Mrs. Molloy.'

'Good. I'll be anxious to hear what transpired.'

Seth was sitting on my porch. 'Any luck?' he asked.

'No. You?'

'You mean did the fish bite?'

'I suppose you could put it that way.'

'Well, Mrs. Molloy and I did have a chat.'

'Glad to hear it. Let me get out of this fishing gear.

'Was she married to the deceased?' I asked after rejoining him on the porch.

'I don't quite know, Jessica. I asked her how long they'd been married. She said, 'Not too long.' I mentioned her grown-up daughter in San Francisco, and she said, 'She's from a previous marriage.' I asked her what her husband did for a living. She said, 'I never really knew.' You know, Jessica, the woman is a mess. Looks to me like she lives on exercise machines and pills. Probably those damn diet pills that make her hyper, and then she comes down to earth with Valium. She's in her own world.'

'That's sad. Did you talk about anything else?'

'*Ayuh*. She asked me to write her a couple of prescriptions. I told her I wasn't licensed to do that in Colorado. That's when she suggested that maybe I could call them in to a pharmacy in Maine and have FedEx fly 'em out here.'

'She's sick.'

'Very much so. Ready for lunch?'

'Yes. But first, let me report on what happened to me.'

I told him of finding the rasp, and that Investigator Pitura had sent it to the medical examiner for analysis. Seth agreed it was strange that the rasp just showed up the way it did.

'Of course, we don't know that it was the weapon,' I said.

He narrowed his eyes. 'But you're pretty sure it is, aren't you?'

'Let's just say I'll be surprised if it isn't. And if I'm right, the larger question is, who wanted it found?'

## CHAPTER ELEVEN

A professional fly fishing expert was scheduled to give lessons at the stocked pond after lunch, but I decided to take a long walk instead. I started out along the road, but didn't get very far. I'd just passed the area where Molloy's body was found when I sensed someone behind me. I turned to see Pauline Morrison, Craig and Veronica's daughter, closing on me. I stopped and waited for her to catch up.

'Hello,' I said. 'Feeling better?'

She looked back toward the ranch, as

though to confirm that no one else was in the vicinity. 'I guess so,' she said. 'I've been acting pretty dumb.'

'Oh, don't say that. This has been extremely upsetting.'

'Evelyn says I'm being a baby.'

'Evelyn? Your grandmother?'

'Yes. She won't let us call her "Grandma." She says it makes her sound old.'

It didn't surprise me that Evelyn Morrison would feel that way, but I didn't tell her granddaughter that. Instead, I asked, 'Feel like a walk? A good walk always clears my head, makes me feel better.'

'Okay.'

We walked in silence for a minute before I said, 'I understand there's a secret little lake with lots of fish. Do you know where it is?'

'Hidden Lake? Sure.'

'I'd like to see it. Take me to it?'

'It's only a half mile. I used to go there last year a lot to get away.'

We took a narrow, steep rutted road that branched off from the main road and followed it until reaching Hidden Lake, a small, pretty body of water owned by Jim and Bonnie, and stocked with fish. It was eerily silent there, the only sounds the rustling of leaves when a breeze came up, and the happy sound of an occasional songbird.

'You said you came here often last year, Pauline.'

'Uh-huh. I always sat over there, on the other side!'

'Looks like a peaceful place to sit and reflect.'

We made our way to the other side, having to step carefully on rocks to keep from getting our shoes wet. Pauline sat on a fallen tree, placed her elbows on her knees, and leaned forward, her head nestled in her hands. I observed her. When we were first introduced, she was a lively, happy girl. But since the murder of Paul Molloy, she'd gone into a shell.

This was the first time I'd seen her since word of the murder spread through the ranch.

I sat next to her. 'Care to talk about it?' I asked.

She replied without lifting her head, 'What's to talk about?'

'The murder. Sometimes it helps to say what's on our minds, to vent our feelings.'

I felt comfortable in offering myself as an amateur therapist because I wasn't a member of her family. It's often easier to discuss intimate thoughts with a stranger.

'I'm not supposed to talk about it.'

'Oh?' I said. 'Who told you not to?'

She shrugged. Translation: I'd better not say.

Our silence melded with the absence of nature's sounds. I looked at her out of the corner of my eye, and was struck again at how physically different she was from the rest of her family. Funny, I thought, how genes work. There can be a succession of children, all carrying strong familial traits, and then along comes another child who looks as though he or she is from a different set of parents. As dark as the rest of the Morrison family was, Pauline was fair, her hair flaming orange, freckles dotting her pretty face.

'Do you enjoy coming to the Powderhorn?' I asked, wanting to break the awkward lull.

'No.'

'Don't enjoy riding?'

'Sometimes.'

'How many years have your mom and dad been bringing you?'

'A couple.' She suddenly stood, turned her back on me, wrapped her arms about herself, and started to sob softly. I couldn't hear her, but could see the movement in her body. I came up behind and placed my hands on her shoulders.

'Just leave me alone,' she said.

I removed my hands, saying, 'I thought you wanted to be with me, Pauline. I thought that was why you followed me on the road.'

She fought to control herself, slowly turned, and said, 'I did. I mean, I wanted to talk to somebody. But I'm afraid.'

'Of what. Of whom?'

'Of—' She burst into tears and stumbled away, her feet sloshing through the water at the lake's perimeter.

I shouted, 'Pauline, I think—'

She pushed through a clump of bushes and disappeared down the narrow road.

The abrupt end to our conversation was unsettling, and I drew a couple of deep breaths before slowly walking back to the ranch, where Jim Cook stood at the entrance with homicide investigator Bob Pitura.

'Were you with Ms. Morrison?' Pitura asked me.

'Yes. She showed me Hidden Lake.'

'She just came running past us,' Jim said, 'crying her eyes out. What happened?'

'Nothing. We were talking. Then she started to cry and took off.'

Pitura looked at me with a questioning expression. I knew what he was asking: Had Pauline told me anything in which he might be interested? I tried to return a nonverbal answer with my eyes.

'Bob told me about your finding the rasp, Jess,' Jim said. 'Looks like it came from the stable.'

'You know that so soon?'

'I went there and checked on the tools. We keep a pretty good inventory.'

'So Joe Walker said.'

'We had three of those rasps. They're special, about the thinnest ones you can buy. One's missing.'

'I'm waiting to hear from the ME once he gets a chance to examine it,' Pitura said. 'In the meantime—'

He was interrupted by Evelyn and Robert Morrison, who approached, stern expressions on their faces.

'Hello there,' Jim said. 'I see some of your family took advantage of the free fishing lesson.'

'I don't wish to talk about fishing,' Evelyn said. 'I understand you've found the murder weapon.'

We looked at each other.

'Who told you that?' Pitura asked.

'It doesn't matter who told us,' Robert Morrison said. 'As we understand it, it was a tool from the stables.'

'It's a little premature to speculate on whether it's the weapon, Mrs. Morrison,' Pitura said. 'Might just be a tool one of the wranglers dropped.'

'Exactly,' Evelyn said, 'dropped by a wrangler who is also a murderer.'

'Now hold on a second,' Jim said. 'Nobody knows whether it is the weapon used to kill Mr. Molloy. And even if it turns out to be, that doesn't justify pointing a finger at one of my staff.'

Evelyn's nostrils flared, and her eyes blazed. 'You have the responsibility for the safety of my family, Mr. Cook. A man has been killed in cold blood, and that murderer is still among us.' She said to Pitura, 'I insist that you stop this ridiculous questioning of my family and focus your attention where it belongs, on the wranglers.'

'We're questioning each of them, too, Mrs. Morrison. No one has been ruled in or out.'

Robert Morrison said, 'As an attorney for Morrison Enterprises, sir, I will hold you and your department personally and legally responsible for any harm that may befall this family.'

'I'll make a note of that,' Pitura said.

'I really would like to know how you found out about the rasp.' As I said it, head wrangler Joe Walker came from the main lodge.

'Joe,' Jim yelled. 'Got a minute?' Walker came to us and tapped an index finger against the wide brim of his black hat. 'Yes, sir?'

'Joe, I understand you were with Mrs. Fletcher when she found the rasp down by the creek.'

'She called me over and asked me to find Investigator Pitura.'

'But you knew she'd discovered it in the grass.'

'Right. Is there a problem?'

'Depends,' Pitura said. 'Who did you tell about it?

Walker shrugged. 'Andy. I think Jon was there, too. I told Joel. Nobody told me not to.'

'No, it's okay, Joe,' Jim said. 'Just trying to figure out how the Morrisons here learned of it.'

'None of this is of interest to us,' Robert

113

Morrison said. 'But remember my warning. You too, Mr. Cook. If anything were to happen to any of us, we'll own this ranch.'

Jim raised his eyebrows, but said nothing.

We watched the Morrisons walk away with the same purposeful strides as when they'd arrived.

'Real pleasant folks, huh?' Pitura said.

'They've never been particularly friendly and warm,' Jim said, 'but nothing like this. Always pretty much kept to themselves, did some riding, some fishing, held their family meetings. But no particular trouble with them. The staff didn't especially take to them, but the tips at the end of the week were always big enough to smooth any hurt feelings or ruffled egos.'

'They're okay,' Walker said. 'A little demanding, but I figure that's what we're here for, to meet guests' demands.'

'That's right,' Jim said. 'Of course, we never figured on a murder happening. Joe, did you tell any of the Morrisons about Mrs. Fletcher's finding the rasp?'

'No. Just some of the staff, like I said.'

'Okay. Thanks. Everything ready for the supper ride?'

'I think so. Joel's got all the cookout stuff packed, and the horses are ready to go.'

'Good. See you later.'

'He's the best wrangler we've ever had,' Jim said. 'Knows more about tending to sick horses than any vet I've known.'

'I'm going to my cabin to get ready for the ride,' I said.

'Good idea,' Jim said. 'I'd better take some video of the folks getting fishing lessons.'

'I'll walk you,' Pitura said to me.

Once there were just the two of us, Pitura asked, 'I have a feeling the Morrison youngster might have said something to you, Mrs. Fletcher.'

'Not really. She's very upset about the murder. She told me she wanted to talk to someone, but was afraid.'

'Afraid of what?'

'I tried to get that out of her, but failed. She said she went to Hidden Lake a great deal last year, as she put it, "to get away".'

'I think *I'd* want to get away now and then from her family,' Pitura said. 'Hard bunch.'

'Yes. Have you interviewed her brother, Godfrey?'

'An hour ago, just before he and his uncle and aunt took fishing lessons.'

'And?'

'Surly kid. A teenage malady these days. Grunted his answers and even laughed a few times.'

'A nervous laugh?'

'I suppose so. He had nothing to offer.'

'I'll bet he knows why his sister is so upset.'

Pitura looked puzzled. 'Murder can upset anyone.'

'But she's upset beyond what might be expected,' I said. 'After all, it wasn't a member of her family who was killed. Paul Molloy was a stranger. They spent an hour together at dinner the night he was killed. No, even less time than that. The two kids left the table as soon as they were finished.'

'Maybe you'll have a chance to talk to some of them on the supper ride.'

'I'll try. Are you coming with us?'

'No. I have to get back to town for a meeting with Sheriff Murdie.'

'About this case?'

'Yes. Dick Murdie is a thorough guy. We meet every day.'

I smiled.

'Thinking of one of Jim's jokes?'

'No. I'm thinking of how surprised I was when I first met the sheriff. He certainly doesn't dress like one.'

Pitura laughed. 'I guess we're a lot less formal out here than where you're from.'

'We're pretty informal back in Cabot Cove, too,' I said.

Pitura laughed. 'Dick says that if he's ever seen in his uniform, it must mean he's on his way to an official event, a funeral, or it's Halloween. He says the Wrangler sneakers he wears make him "official." '

'Say hello for me.'

'I certainly will. Enjoy the ride.'

# CHAPTER TWELVE

'How was your fishing lesson?' I asked Chris Morrison as we gathered in front of the lodge for the supper ride, our every move captured by Jim Cook on videotape.

'Good. The instructor was a nice guy. I never did get into fishing. Too much trouble, all that knot tying and heavy gear. But Godfrey wanted to take a lesson, so I went with him.'

I asked Godfrey whether he enjoyed the lesson.

'It was okay, I guess,' he mumbled, then walked away.

'How's Mrs. Molloy doing?' Seth asked Bonnie Cook.

'All right. She still wants her meals in the cabin, which is fine with us. Joel and Sue are taking turns delivering trays. I wonder whether staying alone is good for her, but that's not my decision.'

'It'll take her a while to come out of it,' Seth said as Crystal, one of the wranglers, suggested we follow her to the corral to get our horses.

'Everybody accounted for?' Jim asked, doing a silent head count.

'Willy won't be with us,' Craig Morrison said.

'He can ride with me in the jeep,' Jim said.

'He won't be with us,' Evelyn said in a tone

that put an end to any further discussion of Cousin Willy.

Jim and another wrangler, Jon Adler, drove two Jeeps carrying the cookout paraphernalia. We mounted our horses and fell in line behind Joe Walker, Crystal Kildare, and Andy Wilson. Walker told us before we set out that it might prove to be a long ride for the less experienced, and that we shouldn't hesitate to ask for a rest stop at any point.

It was a beautiful afternoon, the Colorado sky a deep blue, the sun shining brightly, a lovely breeze tickling our faces as we rode slowly down the road until reaching a fork leading up to the high country. A pervasive sense of well-being consumed me as we navigated narrow, rough trails through groves of aspen and ponderosa pine. Rabbits scurried across our path. A doe observed us from no more than a hundred feet away before loping up a steep grade and disappearing over its rim.

The views became more spectacular the higher we climbed, and a sense of exhilaration set in. I wanted to urge Samantha to go faster, but couldn't, of course, because the wranglers set the pace. Also, it was rough terrain, and I marveled at the horses' ability to keep their footing.

No one said much during the first hour of the ride. Evelyn Morrison led the guests, riding directly behind Joe Walker. She rode tall in the saddle, her back ramrod straight, her rhinestone-studded Stetson perfectly positioned. Andy injected himself into the middle of our line, and Crystal moved to the rear. It was obvious since the day we arrived that Jim and Bonnie ran a tight ship. No one was ever allowed to take a horse without being accompanied by a wrangler, who kept a watchful eye on everyone for signs of fatigue, potentially dangerous horsemanship, or anything else that could put a guest in jeopardy.

Seth was the first to call for a break. 'My back is getting to me,' he told me as he stretched against the pain. We'd reached a small clearing, a perfect spot for a rest stop. We climbed down from our horses and milled about.

'How much farther?' Seth asked.

'Oh, another half hour, forty-five minutes,' Andy said.

'Didn't think it would be this rough,' Seth said.

'We can walk the horses for a while,' Crystal suggested.

'No, that's all right,' Seth said. 'I've come this far on horseback and intend to stay with it. Besides, I'm getting hungry. I can smell a big, fat, juicy hamburger cooked on a grill from here.'

After ten minutes, Evelyn Morrison said, 'I suggest we move on. Perhaps you should have gone with Mr. Cook in the Jeep, Dr. Hazlitt.'

Seth gave her a hard look, managed to haul himself back up in the saddle, and said, 'Let's move 'em out!' The wranglers laughed as we mounted and resumed our journey to where Jim and Bonnie Cook would be waiting.

The final leg of the trip was the most precarious of all. Not that we were in any particular danger. The Cooks would not have chosen such a route. But we did have to go up a steep, rocky incline that traced the contour of a narrow trail, with a steep falloff to our right. As comfortable as I'd become on Samantha, I felt a twinge of fear as I glanced down the slope, and silently urged the horse to stay on the straight-and-narrow. Until the rest stop, Seth had been directly behind me. But when we resumed the ride, the order in which we rode changed. Craig and Veronica's teen son, Godfrey, now rode behind me, in front of Seth.

The head of the column reached the crest and slowly disappeared over it. 'Come on, Samantha, nice and easy,' I said in soothing tones, patting her on the neck. I reached the top, brought Samantha to a halt, and looked down at a sprawling meadow. Although they were still a long distance away, I could see that Jim, Bonnie, and wrangler Jon Adler had set up for the cookout in an area containing tables and benches. Smoke drifted up invitingly from a grill. As I urged Samantha down the gentler incline in the direction of the meadow, I turned to see how Seth was progressing. Godfrey had just reached the crest. He'd been taking pictures with a point-and-shoot camera throughout the ride, and aimed it at the meadow. The shot he took was the last one on the roll. The camera suddenly made a mechanical, whining sound.

'Don't do that,' I said, remembering Crystal's admonition when instructing us the previous morning. My response was obviously too late.

I heard a horse whinny, and then the sound of rocks falling, followed by a voice unmistakably belonging to Seth. 'Oh, no,' he shouted.

I didn't know what to do. Should I try to turn Samantha around and return to the crest of the ridge, or get off and run back? My answer was to yell for the others to stop their descent. I then looked at Godfrey, who was observing whatever had happened behind him with curious detachment, and a sly, disconcerting grin.

I dismounted, handed Samantha's reins to Andy Wilson, who'd heeded my call, and ran up the hill. What I saw hit me like a punch in the stomach. Seth's horse stood passively. What was so upsetting was that Seth wasn't on him.

'Seth!' I yelled.

I ran past Godfrey and his horse to Seth's riderless mount, and looked down the fall-off.

Now my heart beat even faster. Seth was twenty feet down the hill, resting on his side against a slender tree that had broken his fall. He slowly raised his hand to me.

'Thank God!' I said, grateful he was alive.

Andy and Joe joined me.

'What's happened?' Andy asked.

'He must have been thrown,' I said. 'The boy—he took the last shot on his camera and—'

The two wranglers ignored me and scrambled down the hill, grabbing trees as they went. They reached Seth and knelt over him.

'Is he all right?' I asked.

Walker looked up at me. 'He's banged up, but not too bad, I think.'

Crystal came to my side. Walker yelled up to her, 'Go get Jim and Bonnie. Tell them to get to a phone and call for an ambulance.'

I felt totally helpless standing there looking down at one of my oldest and dearest friends, obviously injured, undoubtedly in pain, maybe even with life threatening internal injuries.

I wondered how they would get him up from the ravine. It would take at least an hour for any medical personnel to arrive at the scene, probably longer considering the time it would take Jim or Bonnie to report the emergency.

'Can I get anything?' I called to the wranglers, who sat on the ground next to Seth.

Instead of a verbal answer, Seth responded by struggling to his feet with Andy and Joe's help.

122

'Don't move him,' I shouted.

Seth waved his left hand at me and said, 'Not to worry, Jessica. I'm all right. Just stunned and bruised and—' He moaned in pain as he tried to raise his right arm.

'I think his arm's broken,' Joe Walker said.

I started down the incline, using the trees the way the wranglers had. I got halfway to them when Andy said, 'Okay, Doc, we'll do it slow and easy.'

'Maybe he shouldn't be moved until medical help arrives,' I said.

'I'm not about to stay down here until then,' Seth said. 'All right, fellas, let's go.'

I retraced my steps, pulling myself up tree by tree, until reaching the spot where Seth had been thrown. By now some of the others had come back to witness what had happened. The exceptions were Evelyn, Robert, Craig, and Veronica Morrison, who'd continued on to the site of the barbecue. Those who had returned watched the two physically fit wranglers virtually carry Seth up the hill. When they were closer, I could see the pain on Seth's face, which was scratched and bruised. But he didn't make any sounds of protest, simply grimaced against what he was feeling and allowed the wranglers to bring him to the trail.

'Thank God you're all right,' I said, wanting to hug him, but afraid to hurt him.

'I suppose all this padding saved me,' he said, his attempt at a lighthearted comment falling flat.

Jim and Bonnie had taken two of the Morrisons' horses and rode up to us.

'You okay?' Jim asked Seth.

'Afraid my arm might be broken.'

'Anything else?' Bonnie asked.

'Bumps and bruises, plenty of them.'

'We've got to get him to a hospital,' I said. 'There could be internal injuries.'

'Jon's already on his way back to the ranch,' Jim said. 'He'll call from there.'

'We have to get you back to the ranch, Seth,' Bonnie said.

'Can you walk down to the cookout area?' I asked.

'No need for that,' said Jim. 'I'll bring the Jeep up here.'

'Will it make it?' I asked.

He laughed. 'Piece of cake.'

Fifteen minutes later we'd eased Seth into the jeep's front seat. From the way he moved, it was obvious he'd been banged up more than he, or we, originally thought. Even if his only serious injury was a broken arm, taking such a fall violates the entire body, especially when you're on the wrong side of fifty.

It was decided that Bonnie and the wranglers would go on with the cookout for the benefit of the Morrisons, while Jim and I brought Seth back to the ranch to await the arrival of the ambulance. Although Jim drove slowly and carefully, the trip was rough, causing Seth to moan now and then. But each time I asked how he was doing, he said, 'Doin' just fine, Jessica. Not to worry.' He was a trouper, even going along with one of Jim's jokes.

'See that mountain over there?' Jim asked. 'Know why a fella fell off that mountain?'

'No, Jim. Why did someone fall off that mountain?' Seth and I asked in unison.

'Seems he cloned himself, but his clone turned out to be a foul-mouthed, obscene guy. The original guy tried to talk sense to his clone, but he didn't get anywhere. So he took his clone up on that mountain and shoved him off. Know what happened then?'

'No, Jim, what happened then?'

'The original fella was arrested.'

'Why was he arrested, Jim?'

'For making an obscene clone fall, of course.'

Seth moaned, either from pain or in response to Jim's joke, possibly both.

While Seth and I sat in the main lodge, awaiting the ambulance's arrival, Jim went off to check on Geraldine Molloy. He returned just as the ambulance pulled up, manned by two young med-techs.

'How is she?' Seth asked as the two med-techs gave him a fast once-over.

'I don't know,' Jim said. 'She's not in the cabin.'

'Where could she have gone?' I asked.

Joel Louden appeared from the kitchen.

'Have you seen Mrs. Molloy?' Jim asked him.

'No,' Louden said.

'Do me a favor, Joel, and look for her around the ranch.'

'Sure.'

'You're going to the hospital with Seth?' Jim asked me.

'Yes.'

'I've got to get back to the cookout. Damn, where could Mrs. Molloy be?'

I wondered that, too, but my primary concern was getting Seth to where he could be examined by qualified physicians.

'Ready?' one of the med-techs asked.

'*Ayuh.*'

'Huh?' a med-tech said.

'He means yes,' I said.

We climbed in the back where Seth stretched out on a rolling bed secured to the interior of the vehicle.

'Feeling okay?' I asked.

He nodded, then added, 'I've got a funny feeling about Mrs. Molloy.'

'So do I,' I said. 'But we'll worry about that later. In the meantime, let's get you patched up.'

# CHAPTER THIRTEEN

When the ambulance pulled up to the emergency entrance of the Gunnison Valley Hospital on Denver Avenue, I was surprised to see Sheriff Murdie and Bob Pitura waiting there. A woman was with them. The med-techs helped Seth exit through the vehicle's rear doors; he refused to be carried out on the wheeled stretcher.

'Looks like you've been through a war,' Murdie said to Seth, whose face had swollen over the past few hours, his bruises blossoming into grotesque black-and-blue blotches.

'I feel like I have,' Seth replied, forcing a smile bordering on a grimace.

'Anything broken?' Pitura asked.

'His arm might be,' I said.

'We can talk later,' one of the med-techs said, 'after we get him looked at.'

We escorted Seth inside. The woman with Murdie and Pitura fell in alongside me. 'Mrs. Fletcher?' she said.

'Yes?'

'I'm Nancy O'Keefe, a reporter with the *Gunnison Country Times*.'

'I'm sure you're not here because of my friend's accident. People fall off horses every day.'

'No, I'm not here because of that. It's the

murder that happened at the Powderhorn Ranch.'

'A murder must be big news out here. I understand they're rare.'

'Extremely rare.'

Our entourage reached swinging doors leading to the hospital's treatment rooms, in front of which stood a big, burly physician in a white lab coat. I recognized him as the coroner who'd come to the ranch to examine Paul Molloy's body. He smiled at Seth as he said, 'Never easy for a doctor to be a patient.'

'*Ayuh*. You'll get no argument from me.'

'Well, we'll take good care of you.' He pushed open the swinging doors to allow Seth to enter the treatment area, where two younger physicians waited. After the doors swung shut, the coroner said to me, 'We were never introduced when I was out at the ranch.' He extended his hand. 'I'm Hal Scudari, county medical examiner.'

My hand was lost in his. 'Pleased to meet you,' I said.

'I thought we might grab a few minutes together while your friend is being treated.'

'All right.'

'Mind if I tag along?' the reporter, Nancy O'Keefe, asked.

'Prefer that you didn't, Nancy,' Sheriff Murdie said, pleasantly. 'But stay around. Happy to talk with you when we're finished.'

If she was disappointed, she didn't show it.

She said she'd be in the waiting room, then walked away.

'Nancy's a good gal and a hell of a reporter,' Pitura said as we followed Dr. Scudari to his office. 'She came out here to Gunnison after working for some big-time papers back east. We all trust her. She's never betrayed a confidence.'

The ME's office was small and spartan. The only chair was his, behind a gray metal desk. He dragged in three wooden folding chairs, and we managed to squeeze into the confined space.

'I understand from the sheriff that you've been helpful in his investigation of the Molloy murder, Mrs. Fletcher,' Scudari said.

'I'd like to be, but I'm afraid I haven't produced much.'

'Modesty is always an appealing trait. Bob tells me you discovered the possible weapon.'

'By sheer chance.'

'It doesn't matter how the discovery came about. I've examined the rasp closely and subjected it to a number of tests.'

'And?'

'Mr. Molloy's fatal wound was certainly caused by a rasp of precisely the dimensions and characteristics of the one you found.'

'That's good to hear.'

'But it didn't kill Mr. Molloy.'

'It didn't?'

'No. I could find no trace of blood or other

bodily fluids on it.'

'None?'

'None.'

'Fingerprints?'

'Impossible on its rough surface.'

'So, Mr. Molloy was killed by such a rasp, but not that particular one.'

'Exactly.'

'You're certain of that?'

'Well, a lack of evidence is never as definitive as actually finding some. Always tough to prove a negative. But I would say that the absence of blood on the rasp clearly rules it out as the murder weapon. If it were a smooth metal object, ridding it of blood would be relatively easy. But a rasp has a thousand crevices in which blood can collect. Cleaning it would be virtually impossible. And with today's modem electronic equipment, we can detect even the smallest traces of blood or other fluids.'

'I appreciate being told this,' I said. 'In a sense, I'm pleased with the result. If it *had* been the murder weapon, it would have made it even more remarkable that it suddenly showed up in broad daylight on the grass.'

'I agree with that,' Sheriff Murdie said.

Dr. Scudari added, 'Because I'm convinced the murder weapon was a rasp of the same dimensions and configuration as the one you found, Mrs. Fletcher, it's my opinion that it took someone with considerable strength to drive it into Mr. Molloy's chest. If the weapon had been smooth, say a knife, it would not take excessive strength. But the rasp's rough surface is another matter.'

'That makes sense,' I said. 'But the question then becomes why the rasp I found was placed where it was.'

'Could be that somebody believed it *was* the weapon,' Pitura offered, 'maybe found it in some obscure location and put it where it would be easily spotted.'

'But why do that?' I asked. 'Why not just turn it over to you?'

The large homicide investigator shrugged. 'Perhaps didn't want to become involved. I've seen that happen before.'

I turned to Dr. Scudari. 'Are you saying it would take an extraordinary amount of strength to plunge the rasp into Mr. Molloy's chest?'

'Extraordinary? Super-human? No. But it wouldn't have been a matter of just poking it at Molloy, as you could with a knife. It had to be rammed into his chest, and that would take some force.'

'How far did it enter his body?' I asked.

'Far enough to reach his heart and kill him.'

The sheriff said, 'If you're thinking, Mrs. Fletcher, that it had to be a man, I disagree. It could have been a woman, or a teenager, acting out of rage.'

Scudari nodded in agreement. 'People are

131

capable of remarkable feats of strength when provoked. An extremely angry person, man or woman, can go into almost a trancelike state. The medical literature is filled with such instances.'

The door to Scudari's office opened, and one of the physicians who'd examined Seth poked his head through. 'Nothing broken,' he said, smiling. 'His right shoulder was dislocated, but we popped it back into place.'

I winced at the pain Seth must have felt.

'Doesn't appear to have any internal injuries either. He's just banged up pretty good. He'll have trouble getting out of bed the next few days.'

'I'm glad it's nothing worse than that,' I said. 'Do you think we should leave for home?'

'No,' the doctor said. 'I'd just as soon not see him fly for a while. My suggestion is to have him take it easy at the ranch. No horses, of course. I'll prescribe painkillers. He should be fine.'

The treating physician left, closing the door behind him.

'Anything suspicious about his fall from the horse?' Pitura asked.

I shook my head. 'His horse was frightened by the sound of a camera with an automatic rewind feature. One of the teens on the ride took the last photo on his roll. We were warned about that. I guess he didn't hear, or didn't care.' I recalled Godfrey Morrison's smile after his irresponsible action had sent Seth flying down the slope. Not an especially winning kid, I thought. None of the family was destined to warm the cockles of anyone's heart, for that matter.

Dr. Scudari stood. 'Looks like your friend will be ready to leave in a few minutes, Mrs. Fletcher. It's been a pleasure meeting you. Thanks for your help.'

Sheriff Murdie excused himself, saying he was due at a family event. 'I'll be out to the ranch in the morning,' he said. 'Tell your doctor friend to take it easy for the rest of the week.'

Pitura and I went to the waiting room, where Nancy O'Keefe sat reading a magazine.

'Is your friend all right?' she asked.

'Yes, thank goodness,' I said.

'I'll drive you and the good doctor back to the Powderhorn,' Pitura said, 'unless he needs the ambulance.'

'That's very kind of you. We'll see how he feels.'

'Before you leave, Mrs. Fletcher, could I have a few minutes with you?' Ms. O'Keefe asked.

'Of course.'

'I have some calls to make,' Pitura said. 'I'll see you back here in ten, fifteen minutes.'

'What can you tell me about the murder?' Ms. O'Keefe asked, taking a slender reporter's notebook and pen from her purse.

'Nothing you don't already know.'

'Maybe. Maybe not. You found the body.'

'No.' I recounted for her how Crystal had come upon Molloy's corpse.

'I understand you found the murder weapon.' She consulted notes in her pad. 'A rasp.'

I'd decided before we started talking to not reveal anything confided to me by Sheriff Murdie or Investigator Pitura. If she already knew about the rasp, that was fine. But she'd have to get the word that the rasp wasn't the murder weapon from someone else, someone in authority, not from me. 'You're right,' I said. 'I did find the rasp.'

'Has the ME confirmed it was the weapon that killed Mr. Molloy?'

'Not as far as I know.'

'I've been told that everyone at the Powderhorn Ranch is a suspect.'

'No surprise. Anyone who happened to be there at the time of the murder would naturally be subject to questioning.'

'Including one of the world's best-loved murder mystery writers?'

I laughed. 'Yes, Including her. *Especially* her!'

'What can you tell me about Mrs. Molloy?'

'Mrs. Molloy? I—' I realized that I hadn't told Sheriff Murdie or Bob Pitura that Geraldine Molloy was missing. Perhaps she'd decided to snap out of her grief-driven solitude and taken a walk, a long one.

'The deceased's widow is naturally distraught. She's in . . . she's in seclusion.'

'I made a call about Paul Molloy,' O'Keefe said.

'A call to whom?'

'A contact in Washington.'

'Washington? I thought he was from Las Vegas.'

'He is. But his name rang a bell with me. I couldn't put my finger on it until I dug through some old clips. There it was.'

'There *what* was?'

'A story a colleague of mine had done on Paul Molloy. My friend's a journalist in Washington, was with the *Post*, has been free-lance for a number of years. At any rate, Mr. Paul Molloy was once investigated by a Senate committee—two committees, actually, foreign relations and commerce—about allegations that he was trying to sell weapons to some Middle Eastern countries.'

'Sure it's the same Paul Molloy?'

'Quite sure. As it turned out, the investigation never amounted to much. Scheduled hearings were called off. '

'No truth to the allegations, I take it.'

'No compelling evidence to take it further. But my friend says as far as he's concerned, Molloy was attempting to run weapons, and pretty destructive ones at that, to a couple of nations we aren't exactly friends with.'

'Interesting, Ms. O'Keefe, but I fail to see what bearing that would have on his being killed on a dude ranch in Colorado.'

She laughed. 'And I can't tell you why because I haven't the slightest idea. But, as you say, it's interesting. My friend is going to do some additional checking into Molloy's more recent activities.'

'I'd be curious to hear what he comes up with. Let me ask you something. There's the possibility that Mr. Molloy was killed by someone passing through, a drifter, a random killing. What have you heard on that score?'

She shook her head. 'Nothing. I mean, Bob tells me he's ruled that out.'

'Bob Pitura?'

'Yes. He's pretty open because he knows he can trust me.'

'An enviable position to be in. What sort of paper is the *Gunnison Country Times*?'

'A small town paper, lots of local news. But we go after bigger stories, too.'

'Like murder.'

'Like murder. Especially murder on a local dude ranch of an international arms dealer.'

'*Alleged* arms dealer.'

'Of course.'

Pitura reappeared. 'Ready?' he asked.

'I haven't seen Seth yet.'

'I did. He's waiting for his painkillers. Funny guy, your friend. He says he won't take any medication for pain, but judging from the way

136

he looks—he winces every time he moves—he'll be happy to have them tonight.' He turned to O'Keefe. 'Have a pleasant chat with Mrs. Fletcher?'

'Yes.'

'Come up with any scoops?'

She gave him a sly smile. 'Read all about it in the paper. Thanks for the time, Mrs. Fletcher. Mind if I keep in touch while you're here?'

'Not at all.'

Pitura had been right. Seth looked even worse than when we'd arrived at the hospital. 'Sure you don't want the ambulance to take you back?' I asked.

'I am quite sure, Jessica. Mr. Pitura's vehicle will do just fine.'

We drove back to the Powderhorn in the homicide investigator's large four-wheel drive sports utility vehicle. Although he drove slowly to avoid unduly punishing Seth, the dirt road leading from the highway to the ranch was sufficiently rutted to cause him considerable discomfort.

Bonnie and Jim were at the main lodge when we arrived. 'We kept dinner for you,' Bonnie said. 'Hamburgers from the cookout. We can cook them in the kitchen.'

'Not hungry,' Seth said.

'I'm not either,' I said.

'How are you feeling, Seth?' Jim asked.

'Not too good, but happy nothing was

broken. Dislocated shoulder. Fine young doctor popped it right back in place.'

'Ouch,' Jim said.

'Exactly,' Seth said. 'I think I'd like to get to bed.'

'I'll get you settled in,' I said.

'Much obliged.'

'Before you do, Mrs. Fletcher, could we talk for a few minutes?' Pitura asked.

'You go ahead,' Jim said. 'I'll see that Doc's tucked in and has what he needs.'

'I'll be there in a minute,' I said.

Bonnie disappeared into the kitchen, where the chef, Joel Louden, was cleaning up. Pitura and I went into the large room and sat on facing chairs near the projection TV.

'Yes?' I said.

'I wanted to show you something.'

'What?'

'This.'

He pulled a number-ten envelope from his inside pocket, removed a wallet-sized photo from it, and handed it to me. Most of the lamps in the room had been turned off, and I had trouble seeing the photo. Pitura turned on a light next to me, returned to his seat, and waited for my reaction.

I squinted to bring the picture into focus, holding it this way and that way to gain the best possible view. It was an old color photograph, wrinkled, crinkled, torn, and faded, the colors rendered almost sepia.

'Recognize the person in the picture?' he asked.

'I don't know. The child can't be more than seven or eight years old. She looks familiar. It could be . . . it could be Pauline Morrison, Mr. Morrison's teenage daughter!'

'Looks that way to me.'

I looked at him. 'Where did you get this? Why are you showing it to me?'

'I got it from Mr. Molloy's wallet. Naturally, we went through everything in his possession. Nothing especially interesting in his wallet. Credit cards, some cash, things you'd find in most every wallet. And, this picture.'

'This was in *his* wallet?'

'Yes.'

'Why would Paul Molloy be carrying a picture of Pauline Morrison?'

'Good question. Any ideas?'

'No.'

'But you'll think about it?'

'I have a feeling that's all I'll think about tonight.'

'Good. Then I won't be the only tired one in the morning. Let's get together over breakfast and compare notes.'

'All right. Oh, as Seth and I were leaving the ranch for the hospital, Jim Cook said Mrs. Molloy had left her cabin.'

'Where did she go?'

'No one seemed to know. He had the chef looking for her.'

We went to the kitchen, where Bonnie and Joel were almost finished with their chores.

'I understand Mrs. Molloy is up and around,' Pitura said.

'Yes, it seems that way,' Bonnie said.

'Is she back in her cabin?'

'No,' Joel said. 'We can't find her.'

'How long has she been gone?' Pitura asked.

'It's been hours,' I said.

'I'll go talk with Jim about Mrs. Molloy's whereabouts,' Pitura said. 'I don't like that she's been gone for hours.'

'I think I'll check in on Seth, then get to bed,' I said. 'It's been quite a day.'

'It certainly has,' Bonnie said. 'Sorry for what's happened, the murder, and now Seth's accident.'

'Don't give it a second thought.' Bonnie and I hugged, and I went to Seth's cabin. He'd changed into pajamas and robe and sat stiffly in a chair. I told him that Mrs. Molloy was still missing.

'Should be easy to ascertain whether she left the ranch,' Seth said. 'She couldn't have just walked into town. Someone would have seen a car pick her up.'

'Unless she was picked up down the road, away from the ranch.'

'I just hope . . .'

'You hope what, Seth?'

'I just hope she hasn't ended up the way her husband, or so-called husband, did.'

'That's a grim contemplation.'

'But realistic. You go on back to your cabin, Jessica, and get a decent night's sleep.'

'What about you?'

'Me? I'll be fine. I took one of those pills they gave me at the hospital. It should kick in any minute now, take care of the pain.'

'You're sure you'll be all right?'

'*Ayuh.*'

'I'd feel better if I could keep an eye on you. Want me to stay in the other bedroom?'

'No. You go on back. I'll be just fine.'

I considered sharing with Seth the photo Pitura had given me, but decided against it. I didn't want to do anything that would stimulate him. He needed what sleep he could get that night. Tomorrow would be time enough to tell him about it. I kissed him on the cheek and went to my cabin. I changed into pajamas and robe and was sitting in the living room, staring at the photo Pitura had given me, when I heard footsteps on the porch, followed by a knock at the door. I got up and looked through the window. It was homicide investigator Pitura.

'Sorry to intrude on you like this, Mrs. Fletcher, but I thought you'd want to know that we can't find a trace of Mrs. Molloy.'

'That's troubling,' I said. 'Come in, please.'

'Thanks, but I have to get to town.'

'Any sign in her cabin that she decided to leave?'

'No. Everything's the way it was the last time we went through it, clothes in the closet, suitcases still there.'

'That's even more troubling.'

'Yes, it is. I'm dispatching officers tonight to conduct a more formal search of the ranch and surrounding property. Of course, we'll also check with the airlines, rental car agencies, cab companies, and the like. But if I was betting, I'd say she wandered off on foot and is somewhere in the vicinity.'

'And hopefully alive.'

'That, too. Good night, Mrs. Fletcher. I'll see you in the morning.'

I locked the door and resumed my seat in the living room. My thoughts were many and varied, ranging from dismay at what these events were doing to my friends, Jim and Bonnie Cook, to vivid, unpleasant mental images of Geraldine Molloy being found dead somewhere in the vicinity. I absently picked up the schedule for the next day's events. There would be the morning and afternoon rides, and a fish fry for lunch on the small island on the banks of Cebolla Creek.

I considered reading in bed, but decided not to. Instead, I examined the faded photograph Pitura had given me.

Was it Pauline Morrison as a small child?

I was convinced of it.

Paul Molloy had carried that picture with him in his wallet.

She certainly looked enough like him to be his daughter.

Geraldine, his supposed wife, probably wasn't his wife, and was now missing.

Someone had placed a rasp where it would easily be found, but it wasn't the murder weapon.

A fresh pot of brewed coffee had been in the Molloy's cabin when I went there the morning of Paul Molloy's murder. Yet Bob Pitura had agreed with me that the murder had probably been committed before dawn. Had Paul Molloy made the coffee in the middle of the night before venturing out? Why would he have done that? More intriguing, why had he left the cabin in the first instance? To meet with someone? His killer? One of the wranglers, Jon Adler, said he'd seen a stranger on the road early that morning.

Another wrangler, Andy Wilson, when mentioning he'd been doing his laundry on Monday night, was challenged by Sue, the cabin girl.

Had Paul Molloy been an international arms dealer, as Nancy O'Keefe claimed? If so, what connection might that have had with the events at the Powderhorn Ranch?

My final question before succumbing to sleep was whether any member of the Morrison family knew that Paul Molloy might be the real father of Craig and Veronica Morrison's teen daughter. None of them indicated any recognition of the Molloys when they arrived Sunday night, which didn't necessarily prove that at least one of them knew something about him.

One thought mingled with the next, the questions melding into one large, unfathomable blur, until sleep put it all to rest.

## CHAPTER FOURTEEN

I showered and dressed before sunrise. Despite a lack of sleep, I was brimming with energy—and consumed with questions.

Although the sun had not yet risen, its promise created the beginnings of a dim, gentle light in which the buildings of the Powderhorn Dude and Guest Ranch were barely visible. It occurred to me as I stood on the porch of my cabin that the murder of Paul Molloy had, in a sense, killed a little in all of us. It's one thing to read about someone's murder in the newspapers, or to hear about it on television. That's bad enough. But to have met someone, to have had dinner with him, and then to look down at his lifeless body the next morning, plays havoc with your mind and emotions. It certainly had for me.

There was a pervasive quiet on the ranch that time of the morning. The staff and guests were still asleep. The silence of the horses seemed to say that they, too, recognized it was too early to make their presence known.

I scanned the ranch in search of the officers Pitura had dispatched to help search for Mrs. Molloy, but saw no one. Had they located her while I slept? Was she dead or alive?

I went back inside and retrieved a small pocket flashlight that's part of my standard traveling paraphernalia. I stepped back onto the porch and did another visual sweep of the ranch before going down the few steps and following the road in the direction of the stables. As I passed Jim and Bonnie's home, lights came on. Running a popular dude and guest ranch meant no sleeping in during the season. Their winter hibernation was when they would catch up on sleep, and lots of other things.

I had to navigate a fence and a quirky gate to reach the stables. It also meant crossing the corral and its minefield of horse droppings. I used my flashlight sparingly. Better to have to scrape off my boots than to alert someone that I was there.

I wondered whether any of the wranglers would be working in the stables at that early hour. If they were, I planned to say that I had trouble sleeping and was simply taking a walk. As it turned out, I seemed to be alone except for the horses peacefully lined up in their individual stalls, awaiting another day of transporting guests into the splendiferous

Colorado hills.

I paused at a door leading into the stables, then tentatively pushed it open. Its hinges made a grating, rusty sound, not very loud but magnified in the relative stillness. I drew a breath, turned on my flashlight, and stepped inside. It was pitch-black. A musty odor combined with the smell of horses was surprisingly pleasing.

I played the light on the walls. A variety of tools and gear the wranglers used with the horses was neatly arranged. Twenty feet ahead of me was a room, its door partially open. I took slow, deliberate steps until reaching it and shone the light on a crude wooden sign: TOOL ROOM. I opened the door fully and trained my tiny source of light on a workbench on the far wall. I stepped into the room, went to the workbench, and examined a neat row of wooden boxes lined up against the wall. I went from box to box, using my light to illuminate their contents, until I found the one I was looking for. It contained an assortment of metal files and rasps. I sorted through them, removed the sort of rasps I'd found by the creek the day before, and laid them side by side on the table. There were three, one identical to the next, and to the one I'd turned over to the police.

I picked up the first, trained the beam of light on it, and brought it close to my face. I did the same with the other two. Once I'd looked at all three, I replaced two in the box and wrapped the remaining rasp in a handkerchief.

I was poised to leave when a sound froze me in place. I slowly turned my head in the direction from which it had come, but was faced with nothing but darkness.

'Who's there?' I called out.

'Good morning, Mrs. Fletcher.'

The sudden, unexpected man's voice caused me to drop the flashlight and rasp to the dirt floor.

An overhead light came on.

'Sorry to startle you, Mrs. Fletcher,' Robert Pitura said, stepping into the light from behind a cabinet.

'You scared the wits out of me,' I said breathlessly.

He picked up the flashlight and rasp, and handed the flashlight to me.

'You were hiding there when I came in?'

'Yes. Sorry. I heard someone enter the stable, but didn't know it was you. What are you doing here?'

'I was . . . looking for the murder weapon.'

'The other rasp.'

'Exactly. Is that why you're here?'

'Yes. I see you found it.'

'I don't know whether it is or not. It appears to have stains on it, in the grooves.'

'Oh, I think it is the weapon used to kill Mr. Molloy. I did a pre-emptive. It's blood all

147

right.'

'Why did you put it back in the box?' I asked.

'To see whether whoever came in after me was looking for the same thing. You were.'

'How long have you been here?'

'Most of the night. I went home, but couldn't sleep. I came back with one of the officers.'

'Any word on Mrs. Molloy?'

'No.'

'I looked for your people when I got up, but didn't see any.'

'I told them to wait until daylight. Stumbling around in the dark won't accomplish much. Bonnie and Jim set them up with coffee and Danish in the lodge.'

'Always the gracious host and hostess.'

He laughed. 'You won't find better people than the Cooks. How's your doctor friend?'

'Sleeping, I assume. I looked in on him last night. He was in pain, but seemed to be doing okay.'

'Given any more thought to the photo I gave you?'

'Plenty. The person who might have an answer is Mrs. Molloy, but she's not available.'

'What about the kid?'

'Pauline? I'd be hesitant about broaching it with her. If Molloy *was* her biological father, it would be the sort of shock no youngster needs.But we do need an answer.'

'We? You make it sound as though I've joined the Gunnison sheriff's department.'

'We'd be happy to have you, Mrs. Fletcher.'

We were interrupted by Joe Walker and Crystal Kildare as they entered the stable and joined us in the tool room.

'Good morning,' Pitura and I said in unison.

They returned our greeting. 'Up pretty early, I see,' Walker said.

'That we are,' Pitura said. 'Well, you young folks have a good day.'

We left the stable and stood outside. Pitura stretched and yawned. 'Getting a little too old to be pulling all-nighters,' he said.

Four uniformed officers came from the lodge, led by Bonnie Cook. 'Good morning,' she said.

'You fellas well fed?' Pitura asked.

'Yes, sir.'

'Then let's get to it.' He handed the rasp wrapped in my handkerchief to one of them. 'Run this in to Doc Scudari.' He gave the others instructions on how to proceed with the search for Geraldine Molloy. 'I'm assuming the best case scenario,' he told Bonnie and me. 'But if we don't come up with her by this afternoon, I'll bring in the dogs and the Necro team.'

'Necro team?' I asked.

'Also known as the "pig team." All volunteers. They started out years ago by burying pigs and observing how the soil and

149

plant life changes in an area where something's been buried. Most of them are scientists of one stripe or the other, university professors, lab workers, that sort of thing.'

'I hope she found a way into town and is home in Las Vegas by now,' Bonnie offered, her voice not exuding any confidence in that possibility.

'Sheriff Murdie's already been in touch with the Las Vegas police,' Pitura said. 'We'll find her one way or the other. The sheriff's got a sign over his desk that says, "We will do the impossible at once, miracles take a little longer, magic will be practiced tomorrow." He means it.'

'Will you be riding this morning?' Bonnie asked me.

'I don't think so, Bonnie. I'd like to stay close to Seth. He'll be feeling the effects of the fall.'

'I imagine so.'

As we walked to the lodge, Bonnie asked, 'Mind if I ask what you and Bob were doing in the stables so early this morning?'

'Looking for the murder weapon.'

'Really? I thought the rasp you found was it.'

'Turns out it wasn't. But I think the one we came up with this morning will prove to be. See you at breakfast after I've checked in on Seth.'

To my surprise, Seth was in the shower

when I arrived at his cabin. I waited on the porch until he joined me, wearing a robe and slippers. His face was still black and blue and swollen, and he moved like a person in pain. But his spirits were high.

'You look remarkably well,' I said.

'Lots of aches and pains, Jessica, but not as bad as I thought it would be. Took it real easy getting out of bed. The hot shower felt good. Anything new on the murder and Mrs. Molloy?'

'No. We found what seems to be the real murder weapon.'

'We?'

I explained the circumstances of having met Pitura at the stables, and Seth gave me one of his patented disapproving looks.

'I fear the worst for Mrs. Molloy,' I said.

'For good reason. What are your plans for the rest of the day?'

'I thought I'd stay around the ranch, maybe see if I can talk with some of the Morrisons.'

'The daughter?'

'Possibly. Let me show you something.' I handed him the photo found in Paul Molloy's wallet and offered my thoughts about it.

He handed the picture back. 'Very interesting, Jessica.'

'I thought so. Today is Wednesday.'

'*Ayuh.*'

'That means we have four more days here, counting today.'

151

'We leave on Sunday.'

'That's right. We have four more days to determine who murdered Paul Molloy.'

'And if we don't?'

'I go home to Cabot Cove a disappointed lady.'

'Why is it so important that *you* solve the murder, Jessica?'

'My natural curiosity, I suppose.'

'Might it be this newfound need of yours for adventure?'

'Could be that, too. All I know is that we ended up at Jim and Bonnie's Powderhorn Ranch for a pleasant, relaxing week, and had a murder committed right under our noses. I think it would be helpful to Jim and Bonnie if we wrapped this up before we leave. Besides, Vaughan is always after me to try my hand at a true crime book. Maybe this is the one.' Vaughan Buckley's Buckley House had published most of my mystery novels.

'All I can say, Jessica, is that I'll do what I can to help you.'

'Thanks, Seth. I'm glad you're feeling well enough to make that offer.'

'Just trying to protect my best friend. Leave you on your own, and there's no tellin' what trouble you'll get into.'

I kissed his cheek, smiled, and said, 'That's what friends are for. Feel like breakfast? It's French toast this morning.'

'I believe I do, Jessica. I believe I do.'

# CHAPTER FIFTEEN

Everyone was at breakfast that morning, and the disappearance of Geraldine Molloy didn't seem to have dampened spirits. The Morrison clan knew she was missing, yet they were in an expansive mood, at least when compared to their usual dour demeanor.

'Have they made any progress in the investigation, Mrs. Fletcher?' Evelyn Morrison asked, not sounding as though she really cared as she plucked a grape from a fruit basket and brought it to her lips with precision, pinky extended.

'I believe they have,' I replied.

'They're searching for Mrs. Molloy,' Chris Morrison said. 'No doubt about it now. She killed him.'

'And why do you say that, young man?' Seth asked.

'You'd have to be brain dead not to see it,' Chris said. 'She's taken off because she's guilty. I'll bet even these clowns from the local police know that.'

Veronica and Craig Morrison sat across the table from me. 'Are you going riding this morning?' I asked them, to change the subject.

'I am,' Veronica said.

'Not me,' said Craig. 'Looks like a perfect day for flying. I thought I'd do a little aerial

153

sightseeing. Care to join me, Mrs. Fletcher?'

I glanced at Seth, whose expression said he wasn't in favor of it.

'Maybe,' I said. 'When do you plan to go?'

'This afternoon, after lunch. I'm going in to town this morning.'

'I'll let you know later. Thanks for asking.'

'How are you feeling, Dr. Hazlitt?'

'Fair to middlin'.' Seth looked down the table at Godfrey, whose taking of the last picture on the roll had caused Seth's horse to buck. The teenager smiled and dug into his second helping of French toast. I considered mentioning it, but wrangler Crystal Kildare saved me the trouble by again reminding everyone to not take photos when the roll was close to the end. Godfrey made a sour face and continued eating.

My attention kept shifting to Pauline Morrison. Although the photo given me by Pitura was in my purse, I'd studied it so many times I could see it as though it were on the table in front of me. She sat pensively next to her grandmother, eyes downcast, her pretty freckled face void of expression.

Jim Cook ended breakfast with a joke.

'These two cops were outside a bar late at night waiting to see if any drunks tried to drive. They saw this one fella come out. He appeared to be very drunk. He stumbled around the parking lot, tried his key on several cars, sat down on the ground, got up again, kept stumbling until he finally found his car, got behind the wheel and started to leave the parking lot. By now, most of the other patrons had left the bar and driven off. The cops stopped the guy they'd been observing and gave him a sobriety test. He was stone-cold sober, hadn't even had a drink. He told the cops he was the DD. 'You're the Designated Driver?' one cop asked. 'No,' the fella replied, 'I'm the Designated Decoy.'

'I like that one,' Chris said, standing and slapping Jim on the back.

'All set to ride?' Joe Walker asked.

The Morrisons and the wranglers departed as a group. Joel, the chef, and Sue, the cabin girl, cleared the table while Seth and I had fresh cups of coffee in the main room with Jim and Bonnie.

'No word from the police about Mrs. Molloy?' I asked.

'No,' Bonnie said. 'I almost hope there isn't any news. It can't be good.'

I decided to share the photo with Bonnie and Jim. 'Take a look at this,' I said.

They passed it between them. 'Who is it?' Jim asked.

'I think it's Pauline Morrison.'

'Pauline?' Bonnie said. 'The daughter?'

'Yes.'

'Where did you get it, Jess?' Jim asked.

'Bob Pitura gave it to me.'

'Where did *he* get it?'

155

'From Paul Molloy's wallet.'

Jim and Bonnie looked at each other with quizzical expressions.

'Exactly,' I said. 'Why would Mr. Molloy be carrying a childhood picture of Pauline Morrison?'

'Maybe it isn't her,' Jim said.

'Look at it again,' I said.

'It *is* her,' Bonnie said. 'As a child.'

'What are you saying, Jess, that Molloy could be her father?' Jim asked.

'It's certainly possible,' I said, 'considering their physical resemblance. I was struck when first meeting the Morrisons how different Pauline looks from the others, certainly from her brother. She has the same coloring as Molloy, and there's something about the eyes that's similar. Don't you agree?'

Bonnie said, 'I'm trying to remember what Mr. Molloy looked like. I really never paid any attention. They arrived late, had a quick dinner, and went to their cabin.'

Seth said, 'Any suggestions on how we can find out whether it is the young lady in the picture?'

'Ask her,' Jim said.

'That's too touchy,' I said. 'What if it isn't her? It would be a horrible mistake.'

Seth stood and arched his back. 'I get stiff sitting too long,' he said.

'Are you going to take Craig Morrison up on his offer to go flying?' Bonnie asked as we walked to the dining room.

'No,' Seth answered for me.

I shot him a disapproving look.

'Maybe you'd like a Jeep ride up in the mountains, Jess,' Jim said. 'Pretty day for it. I don't suppose you're up for it, Seth.'

'The last thing I need is to go bouncing around in a Jeep,' Seth said. 'Hurts me just to think about it.'

'I'd love to go,' I said. 'Do you mind, Seth?'

'Of course not. You go ahead and enjoy it. I intend to spend a quiet day on my porch in a rocking chair. You'll be back by lunch?'

'Sure will,' Jim said. 'Fish fry on the island.'

Jim had a few chores to do before we could leave. I sat in front of the lodge and watched some of the Morrison family come from their cabins and head for the corral. Evelyn, dressed in her well-tailored riding gear, stood on her porch with Pauline. Judging from her posture, she was angry at something and was obviously uttering harsh words at her granddaughter. Evelyn stormed from the porch and joined her brother, Robert, who'd just come from his cabin. I watched them go to the corral, then looked again at Pauline. The teenager, head lowered, slowly opened the door and disappeared inside.

I crossed the grassy area, stepped up onto the porch of Evelyn's cabin, and said through the screen door, 'Pauline?'

'What?' she asked. I could tell from her

voice that she'd been crying.

'It's Jessica Fletcher. I wonder if we could talk.'

She appeared on the other side of the screen. 'Mrs. Fletcher, I—'

Her eyes opened wide, and she disappeared from my view. I turned to see what she'd reacted to. Evelyn Morrison stood at the foot of the steps, eyes blazing, lips set in a thin, angry line.

'I saw that your granddaughter wasn't going riding this morning and thought we might—'

'Stay away from her,' Evelyn said.

'I only thought that—'

'She has nothing to say to you.'

'Mrs. Morrison, I—

'Stay away from my granddaughter. Do I make myself clear?' The venom in her voice was palpable.

As I walked away, I could feel her eyes boring into my back. What, I wondered, would cause her to be so strident over my wanting to speak with her granddaughter?

As I passed other cabins, I saw Cousin Willy sitting on his porch.

'Good morning,' I said.

'Morning.'

'Looks like it's going to be a beautiful day. You're not riding?'

'No. I've had it with horses, especially after what happened to your friend.'

'It was a freak accident.'

'Stupid Godfrey did it.'

'Godfrey? Oh, with his camera. He didn't mean anything, I suppose. He wasn't thinking.'

'He never does.'

I laughed. 'Are the police still looking for Mrs. Molloy?'

'I guess so. I saw them a little bit ago.'

'Have they had any luck?'

He shrugged.

He seemed willing to talk, and I wanted to keep the conversation going. 'Mind if I join you?' I asked.

Another shrug.

I sat next to him. He looked as though he hadn't slept much last night. There were dark circles beneath his eyes; a day's growth of beard added to the look of dissipation. He wore a white shirt, gray slacks, and loafers that needed polishing.

'Quite a family you have, Willy. Is Willy all right, or is it William? Bill?'

'Everybody calls me Willy. I hate it. It's William.'

'How are the family business meetings going?' I asked, trying to keep the conversation flowing.

'I don't know. They don't need meetings. They don't include me. Evelyn makes all the decisions anyway. They say they're meeting so they can write the week off on their taxes.'

'Terrible, isn't it, what happened to Mr. Molloy? And now his wife is missing.'

159

'Chris says she killed him.'

'So I've heard. What do you think?'

'I don't know.'

'What does the rest of your family say?'

'Who cares?'

'I just thought—'

'I wish this week were over. I hate it here.'

'That's a shame. It's such a beautiful ranch.' He hadn't looked at me as he talked, as though he were speaking to some unseen person beyond the porch. Now he turned and fixed me with his watery green eyes. 'How come you ask so many questions?'

'Was I? Asking questions? I didn't mean anything by it. Just my natural curious self at work, I guess. Writers tend to be curious.'

'I'm a writer, too.'

'Are you? What sort of things do you write?'

'Science fiction. '

'I'm afraid I don't read much science fiction. Have you been published?'

'No. I don't write what publishers want. I write what I like to write. The publishers don't understand what I'm doing. All they care about is big bucks and big names.' I'd heard that rationalization before from unpublished writers, and wasn't about to challenge him.

'I'd like to read something you've written, William.'

'Would you?'

'Yes.'

'I brought a short story with me.'

160

'Let me see it.'

He returned from the cabin and handed me a manuscript.

'I'll read it tonight,' I said. 'Does your family like what you write?'

He guffawed. 'They don't like anything I do, especially Evelyn and Craig. Always on my back. Don't do this, Willy. Don't say that, Willy.'

I felt sorry for him. He evidently was considered the family black sheep, the loser, a disappointment to the others.

'I'm going on a jeep ride in a few minutes with Jim Cook. Care to join us?'

'I don't think so.'

I saw Jim driving one of two Jeeps out of a garage. 'I think I'd better go,' I said. 'Looks like my ride is ready.'

I stepped down from the porch and was walking away when Willy stopped me with 'That Mrs. Molloy who's missing.'

I turned. 'What about her?'

'I saw her last night.'

I returned to the porch. 'When last night?'

'I don't know. About six maybe.'

'Six? Where did you see her?'

'At her cabin. The honeymoon one.'

'Oh, that's right. You didn't come on the ride. Did you talk to her?'

'No. The cook, Joel, was with her.'

'Have you told the police?'

'No. Why should I? They think I'm a jerk. I

don't want to talk to them.'

'Well, William, you may have to because I'll tell them.'

'That's okay. Hope you like my story.'

I climbed in the front seat of Jim's vintage Jeep, open except for a roll bar above our heads.

'All set?' he asked.

'Let's go.'

As he drove through the ranch's entrance and turned onto the dirt road, homicide investigator Pitura and two uniformed officers came on foot from the other direction. Jim stopped to talk with them. 'Any luck?' he asked.

'Nope,' Pitura said. 'I'm going to call in reinforcements, dogs, the Necro team, probably a chopper, too.'

'Doesn't look good, does it?' Jim said.

'No, it doesn't. Off for a ride, Mrs. Fletcher?'

'Yes.'

'You don't need me, do you?' Jim asked.

'No, you go on. Best to keep things as normal as possible for you and your guests.'

'I appreciate that. We'll be back by lunch.'

We started up a hill on the road we'd followed on the supper ride, but Jim quickly branched off onto an even narrower trail. Bushes on either side were so close we had to keep ducking to avoid being hit in the face by their branches.

'Hope you don't mind a rough ride,' Jim said, continually shifting gears to adjust to the terrain.

'Not at all,' I said, raising my voice over the loud sound of the Jeep's straining engine.

After traveling fifteen minutes, we stopped in a clearing and got out to stretch. He led me to a ponderosa pine tree. 'Watch what happens when I scratch this,' he said, using his thumbnail to dig into the bark. 'Smell it.'

'Smells like caramel.'

'That's right. Some smell like vanilla.'

'It's such a beautiful place you and Bonnie now call home.'

'We love it, Jess. We count our blessings every day.'

Before resuming the journey, Jim pointed out various flowers on the perimeter of the clearing. The variety of color was breathtaking. Since moving to Colorado, my friend had become an expert on local flora and fauna and enjoyed demonstrating it. He pointed out white flowers called bedstraw used by early settlers to pack their mattresses and pillows; wild iris, one of three poisonous plants in the area; Canadian pistils; Indian paintbrush, which Jim said was named for a mythical Indian artist who, legend had it, cried over a slain lover, each teardrop becoming a bush; yellow Powderhorn orchids and sunbursts; violet stonecrop, purple tansy asters, red rose hips, and dozens of others.

'Ready to move on?' he asked.

'What? Oh, yes, of course. I was thinking of what a cruel contrast the beauty of this place makes with murder.'

'I'm trying not to think about it, Jess. Come on. There's lots more to see.'

We drove into an area Jim described as 'BLM' land, belonging to the Bureau of Land Management, a federal agency. He pointed to a grassy patch with multiple tombstones. 'That's the Powderhorn cemetery, Jess. Want to guess how many dead people are buried there?'

I laughed. 'How many dead people are buried there, Jim?'

'All of 'em. We don't bury live people out here.'

The higher we climbed, the more Jim had to maneuver the Jeep to keep it going. It took a few minutes to extricate ourselves from deep mud, and to navigate a particularly steep, rocky incline. But the Jeep came through, thanks to Jim's skillful handling.

'Look,' Jim said, pointing to the sky.

'A bald eagle.'

'We've got a family of them living on the east side of the ranch,' he said. 'They stay with us most of the year. Once the water freezes, they move west.'

We continued our bone-jarring ride, stopping from time to time for Jim to point out something, and to take videos of me admiring the scenery. One of our stops was a former copper mine. 'A town called Copperville was here years ago, sort of a tent city. About a thousand people worked the mines until the price of copper crashed. They bulldozed the mine and everybody moved out.'

'Was there much mining in this area?' I asked.

'There sure was. Gold, silver, tin. The government came in here back in the fifties and found uranium.'

'Uranium? For making bombs?'

'Yup. The government cut all these roads you see.'

'Did they use it?' I asked.

'Evidently not. Cooler heads prevailed and decided we didn't need as many bombs as they originally thought.'

'And this is government land?'

'No, it's not, Jess. This is privately owned.'

'By you?'

'Nope. This piece of land sits between our ranch and the Bureau of Land Management land.'

'Who owns it?' I asked. 'A local?'

'Wrong again. Bonnie and I checked the land records when we bought the Powderhorn. It's registered in the name of a company in Denver. Some sort of real estate trust, I suppose. The V.S. Company.'

'What does this V.S. Company plan to do with it, Jim? Mine it? Build a ranch?'

'Couldn't make a ranch out of it. Too hilly. Mine it? Always a possibility, I suppose. All I know is that since we opened the ranch, we haven't seen anybody here. Probably just a long-term investment. You know, sit on it for fifty years and hope it goes up in value. Ready to head back?'

'Sure. This has been wonderful.'

'I love coming up in the hills, Jess. This is such a special place. In the winter there isn't a sound. The creek is under three or four feet of ice, and the birds are all gone. You can't hear the dogs because they're running on snow. Sometimes I think somebody's behind me, but when I look around, I realize it's just my own blood pressure making noise inside me.'

Before getting in the Jeep for the ride back to the ranch, Jim pointed to snow-capped mountains in the distance. We call that Indian snow,' he said.

Sensing a joke coming, I asked, 'Why do you call it Indian snow, Jim?'

'Well, there's A-patchy here, and A-patchy there.'

'I see.'

'That's the only thing I miss in the winter out here, somebody to tell jokes to. Bonnie's heard them all too many times.'

We knew something was wrong the minute we reached the road leading to the ranch. A marked Gunnison County Sheriff's Department vehicle was posted at the entrance, lights flashing. Another was inside the ranch, but visible from the road. A number of people milled about on the tiny island next to Cebolla Creek, where the fish fry lunch was scheduled.

The officer with the car at the entrance waved us through. Bonnie stood in front of the office. The minute she saw us, she ran to where Jim parked near the lodge.

'What's going on?' Jim asked.

'They've found Mrs. Molloy,' Bonnie said.

Jim and I looked at each other.

Bonnie pointed to the island. 'Over there,' she said, 'in the smoker.'

Jim took long, quick strides to the island, with me close behind. It seemed that every member of the Powderhorn staff was there. So was Seth Hazlitt. 'She's dead?' I said to him.

'*Ayuh*. They found her about a half hour ago. Some of the staff were on the island, getting ready for the fish fry. One of them stumbled upon the body.'

Bob Pitura came to us.

'Who found her?' I asked.

'The cook, Joel. He was down here setting up for lunch.' I looked past Pitura to where Geraldine Molloy's body rested on the grass, covered by a yellow sheet.

'She was in that box?' I asked.

'It's a smoker,' Pitura said.

'For smoking meats and fish?'

'Right.'

167

'Was it going to be used for the lunch?'

'I don't know.' Pitura waved for Jim to join us. 'Jim, was that cooker being used today for the fish fry?'

'No. The previous owners used it a lot, but we haven't since we bought the ranch.'

'Any idea when she was killed and put in it?' Seth asked.

Pitura shook his head. 'The ME is on his way.'

'Two murders,' Jim Cook said, dejectedly. 'I can't believe this is happening.'

Seth slapped Jim on the back. 'Buck up, my friend,' he said. 'We'll get to the bottom of this.'

'It had to have been the same killer,' Bonnie said.

'That's a safe assumption,' Pitura said. 'Excuse me.' He joined his officers searching the island for clues.

I led Seth away from Jim and Bonnie to a place removed enough so we wouldn't be overheard.

'I had a conversation this morning with the cousin, Willy. He prefers to be called William.'

'Does he now?'

'He's a sad individual, Seth—talks as though he's been beaten down by the rest of the Morrison family. We actually chatted for a while. He told me when I was leaving that he saw the cook, Joel, with Geraldine Molloy last night at about six.'

'Hmmm. I wonder if he was the last person to see her alive. You should pass the information along to Investigator Pitura.'

'I will. But first I want to talk to Joel myself.'

'You don't want to step on Pitura's toes, Jessica.'

'I wouldn't think of it. But he did ask me to try to find out more about the people at the ranch, guests and staff alike. I'd like to see what Joel's reaction is.'

Seth frowned and ran an index finger over his bruised lip.

'Bonnie told Pitura that Joel was a last-minute substitute for the regular cook, and that he came from Las Vegas. That's where the Molloys hailed from.'

Dr. Scudari, the Gunnison County medical examiner, arrived in an ambulance and performed his visual examination of Geraldine Molloy before instructing the med-techs to remove the body. He came over to us.

'Hate to keep meeting under these circumstances,' he said.

'How was she killed?' I asked.

'Looks like somebody hit her on the side of the head.'

'A different M.O.,' I said.

'But equally as vicious,' Scudari said.

'Have you found the weapon?' Seth asked.

'I believe we have. It was on the ground next to the smoker. A hammer.'

'A plain, ordinary hammer?' I asked.

'No. A special type used to shoe horses.'

*Another weapon from the stables*, I thought. Only this time it was left at the scene of the crime.

Members of the Morrison family arrived back from the morning ride. They halted their horses and took in the scene on the island, then moved on, following wranglers Crystal and Andy to the stables.

I looked in the direction of the cabins. Cousin Willy's porch was empty, but Pauline Morrison stood on her porch, watching us. A few minutes later, Evelyn Morrison went to her granddaughter, and they disappeared inside the cabin.

Bonnie said, 'Joel is putting together some sandwiches for lunch at the lodge. Obviously, we can't go ahead with the fish fry on the island.' My good friend seemed on the verge of tears. She quickly walked away, replaced by Craig Morrison.

'More bad news, huh?' he said.

'That's an understatement,' said Seth.

'How was your morning in town?'

'I got done what I had to. Do I have a passenger this afternoon, Mrs. Fletcher?'

It took me only a second to say, 'Yes. What time do we take off?'

'Right after lunch. I'm hungry.'

'Murder stimulates your appetite, Mr. Morrison?' Seth asked.

Morrison shrugged his large shoulders and

smiled. 'Going hungry won't bring anybody back, Doc. See you at lunch.'

We watched him swagger away.

'I do not like that man,' Seth said. 'I do not like being called "Doc."'

'That's because he isn't especially likable.'

'Sure you want to go flying with him?'

'I wasn't going to, Seth, but I changed my mind. An hour in the air, just the two of us, is a good opportunity to get to know him a little better.'

'I'd prefer you get acquainted on the ground.'

'Not to worry. Come on. We'll have some tea at the cabin and do a little talking.'

## CHAPTER SIXTEEN

Lunch was a catch-as-catch-can affair, with people passing through at staggered intervals, grabbing a sandwich and a glass of lemonade and taking them back to their cabins. Bonnie reminded everyone that there would be a square dance that night after dinner. I had to admire her for not succumbing to what would be a natural temptation to cancel the rest of the week's activities, considering the events of the past few days.

Seth and I took our lunch at the games table in the large room. He ate slowly, taking bites between reading articles in the Denver Post that was delivered each day. I finished quickly, then wandered into the kitchen, where Joel Louden was busy making two large pans of lasagna for that evening's dinner.

'Not easy changing the menu at the last minute,' I said.

'Not so bad, Mrs. Fletcher. Sort of like having the fish fry rained out.'

'Cancelled by murder,' I said.

'Sounds like a good title for one of your books.' He continued his food preparation.

'Yes, it does. I understand you were the last person to see Mrs. Molloy alive.'

My words stopped him; he slowly turned to face me. 'What makes you think that?'

'Someone mentioned it to me.'

'Who?'

'One of the Morrison family. Don't read anything into it. After all, you were bringing meals to her in the cabin.'

'So was Sue.'

'Who brought her dinner last night?'

'Sue did.' He resumed folding ingredients into the pans.

'I'm only trying to put things into perspective.'

'I thought that was the cops' job.'

'It is. But being a mystery writer, I have this need to tie up loose ends and make sense of murder, if that's possible.'

'Well, Mrs. Fletcher, I hope you succeed.'

'So do I. By the way, Dr. Hazlitt and I are enjoying your cooking.'

'I do my best.'

'I understand you were a chef in Las Vegas.'

He paused, his hands poised over the pans, and then continued working, saying, 'I worked there for a while. Not long.'

'At one of the big casinos?'

'Yeah.'

'The Molloys were from Las Vegas.'

'They were? I didn't know that.'

I didn't believe him.

I also took note how powerfully built he was. His arms protruding from a black T-shirt were muscular, and a sculptured chest and shoulders were evident.

'Well,' I said, 'sorry to intrude on your work. The tuna sandwich was good. Glad to hear you weren't the one to serve Mrs. Molloy's last meal.'

'Going riding this afternoon, Mrs. Fletcher?'

'No. I'm going flying with Craig Morrison.'

He cocked his head and smiled. 'Sounds like fun. I always wanted to fly a plane.'

'I'm taking lessons.'

'Lucky you. Enjoy your flight.'

I rejoined Seth. 'Anything interesting in the paper?' I asked.

'Look at this.'

A short article on Paul Molloy's murder was buried inside the paper. Geraldine Molloy's disappearance was also mentioned, although news of her death would undoubtedly generate a longer story the next day. I felt bad for Bonnie and Jim. Despite having had nothing to do with the tragic deaths of two guests, such unfavorable publicity surely wouldn't be helpful, especially if it was to find broader dissemination through a wire service or national broadcast network.

Craig Morrison entered the lodge. 'Ready?' he asked.

'Fifteen minutes?' I said.

'Sure. Meet you right here. One of the wranglers will drive us to the strip.'

Seth and I went outside.

'No sense tryin' to talk you out of going up in that little plane,' he said.

'No.'

'Hope he's a good pilot, not some daredevil.'

'He must be highly experienced. He flies his own private jet, too.'

'Uh-huh.' He looked up to the ridge of mountains that ringed the ranch. Dark clouds were on the horizon. 'Looks like we might get us a storm.'

I laughed and gave him a look indicating I knew what he was up to. 'Stop worrying.'

'I'm not worrying, Jessica. Think I'll take a nice nap. Check in when you're back.'

I kissed his cheek and watched him head for his cabin. As I did, Sue crossed the grassy area, carrying a huge pile of sheets.

'Need a hand?' I asked.

'No, thanks. I'm used to it,' she said, continuing toward a building next to the lodge in which large, commercial washers and dryers were located. The ranch's only public phone was there, too.

'You know,' I said as she started loading the sheets in the machines, 'I've never known your last name. I just know you as Sue, the cabin girl.'

She laughed and blew a lock of hair from her forehead. 'That's me, Sue, the cabin girl. It's Sue Wennington.'

'Hello, Sue Wennington. Pleased to meet you.'

She finished loading the sheets, turned on the machines, and leaned against one of them. 'I can't believe what happened to Mrs. Molloy,' she said. 'I mean, right after somebody kills her husband. It's scary.'

'It certainly is. How was she acting when you last saw her?'

'Acting? Mrs. Molloy? Like she usually did, you know, sort of out of it, spacey, like she was on something.'

'When was the last time you saw her?'

'Yesterday.'

'When you brought her dinner?'

She frowned and chewed her cheek. 'No. I brought her breakfast.'

'You didn't bring her dinner?'

'I was supposed to bring her breakfast and

175

dinner—but Joel said he'd do lunch *and* dinner. We were sharing the job.'

'Oh.'

Veronica Morrison entered the laundry room and went to the pay phone on the far wall.

'I have to go,' I said to Sue. 'Good to know you have a last name. See you at dinner.'

Craig Morrison was waiting in front of the lodge.

'Sorry to hold you up,' I said.

'No problem, but we'd better get the time in before it rains.'

Jon Adler pulled up in one of the Jeeps. A few minutes later, we were at the grass air strip, where Morrison's high-wing Cessna 172 sat alone at one end of the field.

'I've never flown from a grass strip before,' I said.

'Just a little bumpier than concrete. Want to do the walk-around with me?'

We slowly circled the red-and-white single-engine plane, visually examining its control surfaces, tires, struts, and other components. Morrison opened a small panel and checked the oil. I was familiar with the routine because I'd done it when taking lessons from Jed Richardson in Cabot Cove.

'Everything looks good,' he said. He checked the wind; a stiff breeze was blowing straight at us, which meant we'd take off from this end of the strip, into it. I started to climb

176

into the plane through the right door, but Morrison stopped me. 'No, you take the left seat,' he said. 'I'll fly copilot.'

Once strapped in our seats, he went through a written checklist called the CIFFTRS (pronounced 'sifters'), a mnemonic made up of the first letters of controls, instruments, fuel, flaps, trim, runup, and seat belts. Satisfied that everything was in preflight order, he reached under my seat and came up with the ignition key.

'You're very trusting,' I said.

'Out here I am,' he said. He yelled out his open window, 'Clear,' to warn anyone in the vicinity that he was about to turn over the engine and prop, unnecessary since no one else was there, but good standard procedure. He turned the key and the prop turned. After a few more pretakeoff tests, he turned to me and said, 'Go ahead. She's all yours.'

'Oh, I don't think so,' I said.

'Absolutely. Let her roll!'

Instead of arguing, I drew a deep breath, placed my right hand on the throttle, and pushed it forward. The engine roared, and we started down the strip, bumpy at first, but smoothing out as we gained speed, the plane's wings providing a little lift.

'Rotate,' Morrison said.

We'd reached sufficient speed for me to pull back on the yoke and become airborne. Trees at the end of the runway looked too close, but we were soon in the air and passing over them with a comfortable margin. The exhilaration I'd experienced back home in Cabot Cove when flying with Jed Richardson surged through me.

'Nice takeoff,' Morrison said. 'Let's get up to about three thousand feet and turn on a heading of two-seven-oh.'

I did what he asked. As I banked the plane to achieve a compass heading of 270 degrees, I looked down at the spectacular scenery that is Colorado.

'It's breathtaking,' I said.

'Yeah. Great country. Go ahead.'

'Go ahead with what?'

'With the questions you want to ask.'

'I wasn't aware I had any questions to ask.'

He laughed. 'Don't kid a kidder, Mrs. Fletcher. You came flying today because you wanted to pump me.'

All right, I thought, that's exactly what I'll do.

'Your mother seems afraid to have me spend time with your daughter, Pauline. Why is that?'

He shrugged. 'Mother is protective of everyone in the family. I doubt if she's particularly concerned about Pauline.'

'I disagree. Did you know the Molloys before they arrived at the ranch?'

He looked at me the way a teacher looks at a slowwitted pupil who's missed a simple lesson. 'Of course not. Why the hell would you ask that?'

Should I get into whether Pauline might not be his biological daughter, and mention the photo of her Molloy carried with him in his wallet? I decided not to. Raising such a delicate issue might make him angry—very angry—and since I was in his hands at the moment, so to speak, it was prudent to let it go.

I said, 'I just thought that since you and Mr. Molloy seem to be in the same business—land development, is it?—that you might have crossed paths somewhere in the past.'

'Wrong. Next question.'

'Why does Pauline seem so sad? When you arrived Sunday night, she was a bubbling, vivacious teenager. Ever since Molloy's murder, she's gone into a shell. It's as if she had lost someone she knows.'

I could sense anger building in him.

'I'll take it,' he said.

I removed my hands from the yoke, and he took control, urging the plane into a tight turn to the right. It felt as though we were standing on the wing, so steep was the bank. He cut back on the power and allowed the Cessna to slowly descend until we were no more than a few hundred feet above the tops of ponderosa pines lining the mountain ridges.

'Aren't we a little low?' I asked.

'You see things better down here,' he

answered, a grin on his broad face. Then, in a sudden move, he pointed the nose of the aircraft down and flew between a row of trees, lower than their tops, the trunks whizzing by the wingtips.

My shout was involuntary. 'No, no.'

Ignoring me and still smiling, he followed the contour of a mountain that had been stripped of trees—we were no more than twenty feet above the ground—applied power, pulled back on the yoke, and we climbed at a steep angle. As we lost lift due to the wings' angle of attack, and the plane began to shudder as it approached stall speed, he lowered the nose and flew straight and level.

'I didn't appreciate that,' I said.

Jed Richardson always said that pilots who take novice flyers up and fly recklessly do all aviation a great disservice. I now knew what he meant.

'Shook you up a little, huh?' Morrison said, a smug smile on his thick lips.

'Enough to want to be on solid ground. Please land and let me off. You can continue by yourself.'

'Whatever you say.'

He turned the Cessna until we were on a compass heading leading us back to the grass strip. I was still drawing deep, troubled breaths and was so angry I didn't want to look at him. I peered out my window at the passing scenery below, wanting the time to pass quickly until we touched down.

But a strange sound caused me to turn. Morrison's mouth was twisted open, and his head was leaning to one side.

'Mr. Morrison, are you all right?'

His reply was a groan; his head snapped forward, his chin coming to rest on his chest.

I reached over and poked him. 'Mr. Morrison!' There was no response. His hands had fallen from the yoke, and the plane had begun a slow descent.

I grabbed the yoke and pulled back, too sharply, causing it to lose more altitude. I brought it to a level attitude and frantically searched my memory for what Jed Richardson had taught me.

The first thing was to remain calm. *Don't panic, Jess, I thought.* You know how to fly this plane. It's the same one you've been taking lessons in. It'll fly itself as long as you don't do anything stupid.

I looked at Morrison again; he was in the same position.

I leaned forward and scanned the ground ahead of me in search of the landing strip. One of the things I'd had trouble with while taking lessons was being able to identify airports and runways from the air. Jed assured me that all pilots have that difficulty until they adjust to how things look on the ground from above. I knew it would be especially difficult differentiating the grass strip from

181

surrounding terrain. Everything seemed to meld together from my lofty vantage point.

I was almost over the strip when I realized where it was. I checked my altimeter—I,600 feet. I assumed the wind was blowing from the same direction as when we'd taken off, which meant setting up my approach to allow me to land into it.

'Relax,' I said aloud. I glanced to my right. I didn't know whether he was alive or dead. If he was still alive, I'd have to get help for him immediately—assuming, of course, I managed to land safely.

*This is a heck of a way to fly my first solo*, I thought as I mentally made decisions about how to approach the landing strip. One thing loomed largest in my mind. I had to keep my airspeed above the stall range. And as I turned the plane to fly downwind and parallel to the runway, I realized how menacing the trees were at both ends.

I completed the downwind leg, the runway to my left, made a left ninety-degree turn until the strip was perpendicular to me on the left, then made another ninety-degree turn, putting the runway directly in front of me.

With one hand on the yoke and the other on the throttle, I adjusted airspeed, holding the Cessna's nose slightly elevated to gradually lose altitude.

The trees loomed larger and closer as I continued my approach. Stay above them, I told myself. Don't let the landing gear clip their tops. At the same time, I couldn't land too far down the strip for fear of running out of room and careening into the trees at the far end.

Lower, lower—that's it—clearing the trees—kill any remaining altitude the minute you're over them and stall it out hard—that's it—almost there—pull all the way back on the yoke—kill power—and—

I hit hard, and on one wheel, but the other wheel came down and caught the turf. Keep it straight. Okay, apply brakes with your toes on the rudder pedals, but not too hard.

The trees at the far end seemed to rush toward us, but I brought the plane to a full stop a few hundred feet from them.

I let out a sustained stream of air—and relief—slumped back, and allowed some of the tension to drain from my body. I closed my eyes and started to say an unstructured prayer to someone when applause snapped me out of my reverie. I turned. Morrison was sitting up straight, a big smile on his face. 'Nicely done, Mrs. Fletcher. Couldn't have done it better myself.'

'You aren't ill.'

'Never felt better.'

'You . . . you . . .'

'Easy, easy, Just testing you under fire. Shook you up, huh?'

'I cannot believe anyone would be so cruel,

so callous, so . . .'

'Relax. We'll have to walk back. I told Jon I'd buzz the ranch when we were landing to let him know to pick us up, but the plans changed. Let's go.'

'You are a despicable person, Mr. Morrison.'

His answer was to laugh, turn off the ignition, slide the key beneath his seat, open his door, and climb down from the plane. I did the same. I refused to walk with him and stayed a few feet behind as we set off across the field in the direction of the road. He said while walking, 'Did I kill the Molloys? The answer is no. Do I know who did? No again. Do I know why they were murdered? No, although I suggest you and your police buddies take a closer look at some of the ranch staff.'

I caught up with him. 'Anyone in particular?'

'No. Do I think anyone else will get it between now and Sunday? You never know.'

He stopped. 'A word of advice, Mrs. Fletcher.'

'I'm listening.'

'Stay away from Pauline. Stay away from everyone in my family. The police have questioned us. That's their job. It's none of your business. You're a writer. Stick to making up stories. But stay away from us. Consider it a warning.'

'And if I don't heed your warning?'

He shrugged and set off again. 'Proceed at your own risk.'

We said nothing else until reaching the ranch, where Jim Cook was supervising the splitting of firewood. 'How was your flight?' he asked.

'Uneventful,' Morrison said angrily, walking past him.

Jim looked at me with raised eyebrows.

'Uneventful,' I confirmed.

'See you at dinner?'

'Of course.'

'Don't forget the square dance. We've got some extra guests. Nancy O'Keefe, the reporter, will be with us, and I think Bob Pitura and his wife, April, will be here, too.'

'Should make for a lively evening.'

## CHAPTER SEVENTEEN

There was no sense in recounting for Seth Hazlitt my harrowing, infuriating experience with Craig Morrison. He'd only become upset and want to confront Morrison at dinner.

I spent what was left of the afternoon collecting my thoughts and trying to relax. Ironically, the unpleasant airborne episode had energized me. Anger can do that. His behavior was dismaying beyond words. It was as though, I thought while brushing my hair, that he'd acted out what seemed to be the operative attitude of the entire Morrison family—swagger, arrogance, and disdain for everything and everyone except themselves.

Seth was already at the lodge when I arrived for dinner, watching the square dance caller and his wife, Ken and Kathy Ashwood, set up the turntable and PA system while their two children, Michael and Melissa, busied themselves reading books in the large common room. Bob Pitura was there, too, and introduced me to his wife, April, a beautiful young woman with a warm, legitimate smile.

The *Gunnison Country Times* reporter, Nancy O'Keefe, arrived a few minutes later.

'Good to see you again, Mrs. Fletcher,' she said.

'Same here. Been busy writing about the latest tragedy at the Powderhorn?'

'I've been doing some digging, making a few calls. How was your day?'

'Routine.'

Pitura said, laughing, 'We finally released the Molloys' car to the rental agency. They were getting uptight about not having it back.'

'A rental car?' I said. 'I understood they'd been touring this part of the country for a while. I assumed they were in their own automobile.'

'No,' Pitura said. 'They rented it in Gunnison.'

'When?' I asked.

'Sunday.'

'The day they arrived. What did they do, fly into Gunnison?'

'Evidently. We haven't checked that. Should we?'

'Oh, I don't know. I was just thinking out loud.'

The expression on Pitura's face said he'd be checking how the Molloys arrived in Gunnison at the first possible opportunity.

The wranglers and other staff drifted in. The discovery of Geraldine Molloy's body in the smoker on the island had put everyone in a somber mood. It was as though to exhibit spirit was to defile the dead.

But Jim Cook, bless him, wasn't about to allow that sober mood to prevail, not on square dance evening.

'This couple was expecting twins. The husband was out of town on business the day his wife delivered, and his brother took her to the hospital. The new father called the hospital and asked his brother how everything was. The brother told him he was now the father of twins, a boy and a girl. "The doctor asked me what the babies' names would be," the brother said. "I told him the girl's name was Denise." "What about the boy?" the father asked.'

Jim looked at us. Seth and I asked, 'What was the boy's name, Jim?'

'Denephew, of course.'

There were as many moans as laughs, but the tension had been broken, just in time for some of the Morrisons to arrive and cast a new pall over the room.

Joel Louden and Sue Wennington emerged from the kitchen, carrying two large salad bowls. The lasagna couldn't be too far behind.

'You didn't tell me about your flying lesson,' Seth said to me.

'It was fun. I learned a lot.'

'Did you?'

'I'll fill you in later.'

'Why do I have the feeling that it wasn't wonderful?'

'Just your natural suspicious nature at work.'

Craig Morrison and his wife, Veronica, came up to us. 'Did your friend tell you how I almost gave her a heart attack?' Craig asked, grinning.

'No, she did not,' Seth said.

'Tell him about it, Mrs. Fletcher.' To Seth he said, 'Had her baptism under fire, Doc. Came through with flying colors.'

They walked away.

'What's this all about?' Seth asked sternly.

Nancy O'Keefe joined us before I had to answer. 'I've done a little follow-up on Paul Molloy's background in Washington,' she said.

Seth's expression was quizzical.

'Excuse me,' I told him, then followed O'Keefe to a secluded corner.

'What have you learned?' I asked her.

'Nothing that would stand up in court,' she said. 'There wasn't enough hard evidence for the Senate committees to ask the Justice Department to indict. But it seems he was involved with some sort of group that was negotiating with the Libyans to sell them bomb-making materials.'

'That's serious.'

'Yes, it is. I'm working on it from a local angle.'

'Is there one?'

'It looks that way. The group Molloy was allegedly involved with operated out of Denver.'

'I suppose that's local enough. Is there anything that might have bearing on his murder here in Powderhorn?'

'Nothing yet.'

'What about this Denver group?' I asked. 'Who were they?'

'Some shady characters, international traders, wheeler-dealers. The names didn't mean anything to me. There was a woman involved.'

I thought back to Chris Morrison's comment earlier in the week: *'Cherchez la femme*—Look for the woman.' It made sense in murder cases, but an international cabal to sell bomb-making supplies to a rogue foreign state? That would represent a new use of the phrase.

'Her name was Veronica. I remember it because I'm a fan of old movies, especially Veronica Lake films. Remember her, with the blond hair falling over one eye?'

'Of course I do. What was this Veronica's last name?'

'Not as poetic as Lake. Veronica Schwinn.'

'Was she ever indicted?'

'None of them were.'

Nancy's mention of a woman named Veronica caused me to look to where Veronica Morrison talked with her husband and two children, Godfrey and Pauline. I wasn't thinking, even remotely, whether there was some link between these two Veronicas. But I knew few women named Veronica, and it was natural for the thought to make a fleeting appearance. What surprised me was that Pauline was there. I'd come to the conclusion that she'd be kept under wraps for the duration of the week.

'Thanks for the update,' I said to Nancy as Bonnie spirited her away. I rejoined Seth and the Pituras, who were talking with the square dance caller and his wife.

'A pleasure to meet you,' Kathy Ashwood said. 'I'm a big fan of your books.'

'Thank you.'

'Glad to see that Jim and Bonnie decided to go ahead with the dance,' Ken Ashwood said. 'I thought they might cancel, considering what's been happening here.'

'I give them credit for trying to keep things as normal as possible,' I said. 'It can't be easy to put on a pleasant face when you're surrounded by murder.'

Evelyn Morrison made her entrance just as Jim announced that dinner was served. She took her customary place at the head of the extended table and spread her napkin on her lap with a flourish.

'Excellent lasagna,' Seth announced. 'My compliments to the chef.'

'Best I've ever had,' Chris Morrison said, licking his lips. 'Right, Marisa?'

His wife, a woman of few words, nodded.

Bob Pitura was asked about his investigation, but he had little to offer, deflecting the inquiries with a smile and a 'Nothing new on that front' response.

Immediately following dessert, Jim and the wranglers began to move tables and chairs from the dining room in preparation for square dancing. Once the room was cleared, Ken Ashwood said into the microphone, 'All right, ladies and gentlemen, it's time to grab your partner and dance.'

Neither Seth nor I had square-danced in years.

'Feel up to it?' I asked him, thinking of his bruises from the fall.

'*Ayuh*. Lookin' forward to it.'

As much fun as the dancing was, it proved to be more strenuous than I'd remembered. Of course, I was also a little—read 'considerably'—older than the last time I'd tried it. I sat out a few of the dances, some of which were incredibly complicated despite the caller's expert instructions. Seth participated in every dance and seemed to be enjoying himself. Jim, of course, kept the video camera rolling.

During one of my breaks I found myself focusing on each person in the room and what I knew about them.

Joel Louden, the cook, like the rest of the staff, danced with enthusiasm. He'd lied to me about having served dinner to Geraldine Molloy the night of her murder. Why would he have done that? Delivering a tray of food wouldn't cast undue suspicion on him. The worst that would have happened was to be asked about her mood and activities. Also, I thought of his fortuitous arrival at the Powderhorn Ranch the day the regular chef had left. And, he was from Las Vegas, where the Molloys had lived.

Pitura had ascertained that Paul Molloy lived as a bachelor there, yet Geraldine was introduced as his wife. Nothing especially unusual about that in this day and age of unmarried people living and traveling together. Still, I questioned it. From my brief encounter with him, he didn't seem like a man who would be embarrassed to share a room with a girlfriend.

Pauline was next on my visual scrutiny list. I felt handcuffed in pursuing my thesis that she might be the biological daughter of Paul Molloy. With nothing more to go on than that she looked somewhat like him, and more important, that he carried her childhood picture in his wallet, it would have been insensitive, to say the least, to ask the question directly. But I knew that if I didn't, I'd never know the answer. It wasn't a soap-opera interest on my part. If she was Molloy's daughter, it could have a direct bearing upon Molloy's murder.

I shifted attention to Chris Morrison, the younger brother, and his taciturn wife, Marisa. Neither struck me as people who might kill someone. Of course, over many years of being involved with murder, I'd learned that judging people in this subjective way could be foolhardy. What was lacking with Chris and Marisa was a motive, unless it harkened back to some deep, dark family secret involving Paul Molloy.

The reporter, Nancy O'Keefe, who'd hooked up with Seth in a complex dance, laughed heartily as he failed to navigate some of the trickier moves called by Ken Ashwood. According to Nancy, Molloy, a self-professed land developer, was also an alleged international dealer of weapons of potential mass destruction. The Morrison family enterprise was involved in land development, too, and was from Denver where, according to O'Keefe, the arms cabal had been headquartered. One of its members was a woman named Veronica—Veronica Schwinn.

I took in the staff, who were having a wonderful time. Both Paul and Geraldine Molloy had been killed by tools from the stable. Naturally, anyone on the ranch, including guests, could have taken those tools and used them for murder. For that matter, any resident of the town of Powderhorn and surrounding towns could have done the same. The Morrisons were quick to point a finger at the ranch's staff, a little too quick, perhaps.

Aside from Joel Louden's being from Las Vegas, I wondered whether any other members of the staff knew one or both of the Molloys before their arrival at the Powderhorn.

Chris Morrison had come to the immediate conclusion that Geraldine Morrison had killed her husband. But her murder obviously dashed that theory.

Or did it? That theory was based upon a snap judgment that both murders had been committed by the same person. Not necessarily so. It was possible that Geraldine killed her husband, and then was murdered herself by someone else. But I doubted it. I'd reached a conclusion, unsubstantiated by facts, that both Mr. and Mrs. Molloy had been killed by the same individual.

Craig and Veronica Morrison were a handsome couple, self-assured and comfortable with being treated with deference by lesser mortals. Craig was now a known quantity to me, an unpleasant man who found it funny to have someone think he'd died, and then place that person in a frightening situation. Take that sort of warped view of life and extend it a little, and you have someone capable of inflicting any level of cruelty.

As for Veronica, she was an unknown entity. I easily dismissed her as a suspect because she wasn't even at the ranch on the Sunday night Paul Molloy was murdered. I saw her arrive by limousine Monday afternoon. What stuck in my mind was that snippet of conversation between Evelyn and Craig Morrison about her. It was clear Evelyn thought little of her daughter-in-law, and judging from Craig's response, he wasn't sufficiently enamored of his wife to mount a defense of her. But maybe no one dared challenge the family matriarch, even when it involved a person you supposedly loved.

Cousin Willy—whom I would call William from now on—was present at the square dance, but did not participate. He sat in a corner near the caller and sipped a soft drink. What role might he have played in the murders? He didn't seem the killing type, although a lifetime of being degraded and dismissed could turn anyone's feelings into a murderous rage. I surmised that he was the family whipping boy, its gofer, someone who would do whatever he was told. Would that include murdering on the family's behalf?

I looked again at Joel Louden. He'd lied to me about having been the last person to see Geraldine Molloy alive. But I'd come to that conclusion based solely upon William telling me he'd seen Louden with Mrs. Molloy the night of her death, and before Sue Wennington had confirmed it. It isn't like me to make judgments based upon a single source. Was I slipping? I hoped not.

The Morrison children joined their parents in a few dances, but sat out most of them. It was inconceivable to me that either of them would commit murder. But they were old enough. Besides, recent headlines seemed filled these days with tales of youngsters killing people. They shared their own cabin, which meant only they would know of each other's movements. No, I decided. I could accept one of them lashing out at a family member out of extreme anger, but not committing the murders of Paul and Geraldine Molloy.

Who did that leave?

Jim and Bonnie Cook.

Seth Hazlitt and yours truly.

Wrong.

There was also Evelyn Morrison and her brother, Robert.

Killing someone would have meant dirtying

Evelyn's hands, something I was certain she would never allow to happen. But people like Evelyn were used to commanding others to do their dirty work.

It was possible that Robert, an attorney with a sour disposition, shared the view of too many lawyers that because he knew the law, he was free to break it.

My mental exercise was interrupted by Seth. He sat heavily in a chair, wiped sweat from his face with a handkerchief, and caught his breath. 'Haven't had this much exercise in years,' he said.

'You look like you're enjoying it,' I said. 'No aches and pains from the fall?'

'Plenty of 'em, Jessica, but I decided I wouldn't let that hamper me. Care to dance the next one?'

'Sure.'

The square dance ended an hour later. Everyone seemed happy, even the vinegary Morrisons. Bob and April Pitura stopped on their way out. 'I'll check first thing in the morning on how the Molloys got to Gunnison,' he said.

'Good. I'll be interested in what you find out.'

'Enjoy yourselves?' Bonnie asked as the Pituras left the lodge, and Seth and I also prepared to leave.

'Very much,' Seth said.

'Riding tomorrow, or going on the raft trip?'

'That's tomorrow?' I said. 'I haven't even thought about it.'

'We need to know tonight,' Bonnie said.

I looked at Seth. 'Game?' I asked.

'I don't think so,' he said. 'But now that you're into adventure, I'd be shocked if you didn't.'

Bonnie laughed. 'I didn't know you were into adventure, Jess.'

'I suppose I am. That's why I took up flying.'

'How was your flight with Craig?'

'Uneventful.'

'Lacking in adventure?'

'I suppose you could say that. I think I'll shock my good doctor friend here and pass on the raft trip. I need a day just to laze around, nap, read a book.'

'Okay. Sleep tight, you two.'

'I'm certain we will,' Seth said, 'after this workout. Good night, Bonnie.'

We paused in front of Seth's cabin.

'So, tell me about your airplane ride with Mr. Morrison. And don't tell me it was uneventful. I heard what he said, that he almost gave you a heart attack.'

'Actually, I thought *he'd* had one.'

'You don't say. Tell me more.'

We went inside, and I recounted my afternoon's experience. Predictably, Seth was furious.

'It's over,' I said. 'Here I am in one piece and very much alive. I told Morrison what I thought of his stupid stunt. I'd just as soon leave it at that.'

'As you wish, Jessica, but I think the moron ought to be reported to the proper authorities. The FAA. Some agency that can take his license away.'

'We can talk about that in the morning. In the meantime, I'm ready for bed.'

'Jessica.'

'Yes?'

'I've come to a conclusion about who killed the Molloys.'

'I'm suddenly wide awake.'

'I don't think it was anybody at the ranch. I think there's a madman in the area, a serial killer.'

'Who just happened to pick a husband and wife?'

'*Ayuh*. They were both simply out and alone in the wrong place at the wrong time.'

'Interesting theory,' I said. 'Don't lose your thoughts, Seth. Write them down.'

'I'll do just that.'

'Good. Get to bed, and don't square dance in your sleep.'

'I wasn't very good at it when I was awake. Don't suppose I'll be any better in my sleep. I'll walk you to your cabin.'

'Not necessary.'

'It certainly is, Jessica, with a demented killer on the loose.'

By the time I fell asleep, I knew two things.

Seth was wrong.
And I wished he were right.


# CHAPTER EIGHTEEN

When I got up Thursday morning, Socks, the black-and-white border collie, was waiting on my porch, stick in mouth.

'Good morning,' I said.

He wagged his tail and lifted his head to offer me the stick.

'Oh, no. Go find another patsy.'

He ran off the porch and disappeared up the road.

I'd slept fitfully. As much as I dismissed Seth's thesis that the Molloys had been murdered by a deranged stranger, I couldn't get the image of such a person out of my mind. He—and my serial killer was a he—had long fangs, crazed white eyes, and drooled at the mouth. 'Silly,' I repeatedly told myself while tossing and turning. But that didn't do much good, and I awoke fatigued, as though I hadn't slept at all.

I showered, dressed, and took a walk before breakfast. The staff was busy getting ready for another day at the Powderhorn. I stopped to look at the small island where Geraldine Molloy's body had been found. It was cordoned off with yellow crime scene tape, and a uniformed officer stood watch.

I was heading back to the cabin when a small object flew past my head, followed by Socks and Holly. Socks retrieved the stick that had been thrown by William, aka Cousin Willy, and returned it to him.

'Sorry,' he said as he grabbed the stick from Socks's mouth and threw it again.

'The Cooks don't want guests playing with Socks,' I said.

'So what? There's nothing else to do around here. Did you read my story?'

'No, I'm sorry to say. There was the square dance and—'

'Forget it. You won't like it anyway.'

'I'm sure I will. Have you seen Veronica this morning?'

'No. Why?'

'I wanted to talk to her about something. I think we have a mutual friend.'

'Yeah? Who?'

'Someone who knew her before she married your cousin Craig. What was her maiden name? It's on the tip of my tongue but—'

'Schwinn.'

'That's it. Like the bike.'

'Yeah. Like the bike.'

'Thanks. Are you going on the raft trip?'

'No. That's for the kids. I've got other things to do.'

He walked away, and I was now able to vent my exhilaration.

I'd been thinking since getting up about what Nancy O'Keefe had told me at the square dance, that the Denver group involved with Paul Molloy to sell bomb-making materials to Libya had included a woman named Veronica Schwinn. I hadn't planned to pursue it until bumping into William. My question about Veronica Morrison's maiden name had just come out, a spur-of-the-moment, impetuous act not destined to result in anything.

But it had. There was now a firm link between at least one member of the Morrison family and Paul Molloy.

My mind raced as I entered my cabin. Molloy and Veronica had been involved in a nefarious business undertaking. The next obvious question was whether that business relationship had extended to a romantic one, perhaps resulting in a child named Pauline.

If that was the case, it provided motive for someone like Craig Morrison to kill the man who'd had an affair with his wife, and fathered a child by her. And if that was so—and I had nothing to prove it—why would he also kill Molloy's wife? Strike that. Kill Molloy's girlfriend, Geraldine?

I then questioned why I'd immediately looked to Craig Morrison. Any member of the family might have killed Molloy to gain revenge for his having fathered an illegitimate child. The Morrison family was obviously a strong, centered one. Evelyn, the titular head, was capable, I was sure, of going to any lengths to right a perceived wrong.

I realized that I was focusing almost exclusively on a personal motive for killing Paul Molloy. To what extent did their tangled business relationship play a part?

I was enmeshed in these thoughts when Seth knocked on my door. 'Come on in,' I yelled.

'Ready for breakfast?' he asked.

'Yes. You look spry and full of energy.'

'Never felt better, Jessica.'

'Ranch life seems to agree with you.'

'It seems to, especially now that I know none of my fellow guests, or the young folks serving us, murdered anybody.'

'That is comforting,' I said. 'Care to hear another possible scenario?'

'Always open to conflicting viewpoints.'

'Yes, you always are, Seth. Sit down. I want to run something by you, see what you think.'

\* \* \*

'Delicious breakfast, Bonnie,' Seth said after we'd finished a breakfast of Mexican eggs, bacon, flour tortillas, and a cream cheese coffee cake with honey for dessert.

'I'll have to have every piece of clothing I brought on the trip let out when we get home,' I said.

'Or buy a new wardrobe,' Bonnie said with a

chuckle.

I stood with Seth and Bonnie in front of the lodge.

'Looks like it's going to be a fat day,' Bonnie said, using a favorite Maine expression for good weather. The sun was shining brightly, and a cool northwest breeze rustled trees and kissed our faces.

'Looks that way,' Seth said.

Jon Adler, the wrangler who seemed to do most of the shuttling between the ranch and Gunnison, pulled up in the large suburban vehicle. 'Good morning,' he said.

'Good morning.'

'How many are going rafting?' Jon asked Bonnie.

'Down to just three, the two teenagers and their uncle, Robert. Two others cancelled.'

'I'll get this beast gassed up. Are we leaving at nine-forty-five?'

'Yup,' said Bonnie. 'Sure you don't want to go, Jess? Jon drops you where you cast off, then meets you about noon at the other end of the river with a picnic lunch. You'd be back by two-thirty.'

'No thanks, Bonnie.'

I didn't mention that I considered going when I heard that Pauline would be on the trip. But having her uncle, Robert, along dashed the idea. I wanted to get Pauline alone again, just the two of us, and ask a few pointed questions, maybe even whether she knew whether Paul Molloy was her natural father, provided I could muster the courage to do it.

'See you at lunch,' Bonnie said, spotting Jim striding toward the stables and running to catch up with him.

'Lots of work running a dude ranch,' Seth said.

'It certainly is. Feel like a walk?'

'Not particularly.'

'I think I will, walk off the breakfast.'

He laughed. 'It was so good I'd like to hold on to it as long as possible.'

I checked my watch. It was eight-thirty. Hidden Lake was a fifteen-minute brisk walk. I set off at a power-walk pace, which I often do at home. It was a perfect morning for walking, not hot or humid. As I filled my lungs with Colorado's pristine air, a general feeling of well-being gripped me, as it usually does under such circumstances. I reached the lake in thirteen minutes, breathing hard but feeling good. I leaned against a tree for a minute, then circumvented the lake until coming to where Pauline said she came 'to get away.' I sat on the largest rock there, one I assumed she used when seeking solitude, and tried to imagine what was going through her young mind.

A fish broke the water to snare an insect, leaving a series of concentric circles. A rabbit appeared on the far shore, looked around, then scurried beneath a bush. Birds sang. I could see why Pauline chose this particular place for repose.

I sat there until nine, stood, and was about to head back to the ranch when I stepped on a loose rock, lost my balance, and fell to my knees, my hands instinctively reaching out to break the fall. I laughed. *Clumsy you*, I thought.

I started to push myself upright when my right hand touched something unusual. It wasn't a rock or a piece of wood. It felt like metal. I stayed on my knees and wrapped my hand around it. It was metal, a silver case of some kind, not very large, maybe eight inches by six inches. I sat on the rock again and examined it. It appeared to be the sort of container for ammunition I'd seen in the homes of friends back home who are hunters. It had a latch that secured its cover. The latch was slightly rusted, and I had some difficulty opening it. There were no bullets inside. Instead, there was a slim diary. On its cover was written: PROPERTY OF PAULINE MORRISON.

Under ordinary circumstances I wouldn't have even considered opening it. But this was no ordinary circumstance.

She hadn't written much in it, her words occupying only a dozen pages. I read her entries quickly, replaced the diary in the case, closed it, and returned it to where I'd stumbled, literally, upon it.

I reached the ranch at nine-thirty. Jon Adler

was waiting in the suburban in front of the lodge for the two Morrison children and their uncle to appear. Bonnie and Jim were inside doing paperwork on one of the dining room tables: 'More room to spread out here,' Jim explained. 'Enjoy your walk?'

'Yes. It was invigorating, so much so I'm already thinking of a nap.'

'That's what a week here should be, Jess,' Bonnie said. 'Seven days to do whatever you want, when you want to.'

'Thanks for the permission,' I said, laughing.

Bonnie and I stepped out of the lodge as Pauline and Godfrey Morrison left their cabin and came to the suburban.

'All set?' Jon asked, tossing small bags they carried into the backseat.

'I guess so,' Godfrey said.

'Where's your uncle?'

'He's not coming,' Pauline said. 'He has a toothache.'

'A bad one?' Bonnie asked.

'He says it hurts a lot,' Godfrey said.

'I'll go see if I can do anything for him, maybe call a dentist in town.'

'You two are going rafting alone?' I asked.

They nodded.

'It's not dangerous,' Jim, who'd joined us, said. 'The Gunnison River is easy Class Two-Plus water, mostly smooth with a few mild rapids. A scenic trip more than

207

adventuresome. Takes two hours. The guides from Scenic River Tours are all pros.'

'You're sure your uncle isn't coming?' I asked.

More nods.

The kids climbed in the vehicle and Jon started the engine.

'I've changed my mind,' I told Jim. 'Can I still go?'

'Sure. Jon's got extra food for the picnic. Grab what you want to take with you from the cabin.'

'I have everything I need,' I said. 'Let's go.'


## CHAPTER NINETEEN

The professionalism of our guide that morning, Dick Mann, was evident in the thorough briefing we received at the launch area. He went over everything that could possibly happen, told us the commands he would give, and together with his partner, Anne, made sure our flotation devices were properly fitted and secure.

'All set?' he asked as Jon Adler videotaped us from the bank of the Gunnison River.

Pauline and Godfrey said nothing. 'I'm ready,' I confirmed.

The two-hour trip down the river was precisely as Jim Cook had described it. There were a few rapids in which the guide shouted instructions on how to use our paddles to navigate them, but mostly we drifted slowly, taking in the sheer bluffs lining the river, and observing points of interest Dick pointed out. He mentioned that there were a number of other rivers in the area that afforded greater rafting challenges, including the Upper and Lower Taylor, Pine Creek, and the Arkansas, but that the Gunnison was one of the more scenic trips.

Two hours later, we set ashore. Jon was there waiting, Jim Cook's video camera on his shoulder and rolling.

I realized on the ride to town that I might not have an opportunity to find private time with Pauline. Godfrey was ever present, the guide was with us on the river, and Jon Adler was there at the end. Still, I hoped there would be even a few minutes to speak with her alone.

Bonnie had packed an elaborate picnic spread, which Jon laid out on one of two picnic tables nestled in a grove of trees. The Morrison kids said little during lunch and sat apart from Jon and me. Most of my conversation was with Jon, a bright, pleasant young fellow spending his summer at the Powderhorn to earn money for his senior year at the University of Alabama.

As we were about to pack up, I leaned close to him and said in a quiet voice, 'I wonder if there's some way for me to have a few minutes alone with Pauline. I need to speak with her without her brother present.'

'Is this about—?'

'About the murders? No.' I smiled to reinforce my lie.

'Let's see. Yeah, I can take Godfrey down to the river and show him some aquatic life. I mean, if he's interested.'

'Good. Give it a try.'

Fortunately, Pauline took that moment to go to a public lavatory fifty yards away. Jon and Godfrey headed for the river. I didn't know how long Jon could keep the youngster occupied, but hoped it would be long enough for Pauline to return and for me to ask my questions.

It worked out that way. Pauline came to the table. 'Where's Godfrey?' she asked.

'Down at the river with Jon. He wanted to show him something. Pauline, I'm pleased . . . I, well, I wanted to have a few minutes with you alone.'

She looked blankly at me.

'Did you know Mr. Molloy before he came to the ranch Sunday night?'

'Know him? No.'

'But did you know who he was? Did you know he might be—?'

She turned from me and put her index finger in her mouth, clamping down on it.

'Let me show you something.' I pulled her childhood picture from my shoulder bag and placed it on the table. She glanced at it, turned away, then returned to it.

'Where did you get that?' she asked angrily.

'From Mr. Molloy's wallet. The police gave it to me.'

'He had this?'

'Mr. Molloy? Yes. The question is why?'

She placed her hand over the photo, looked at me, and her eyes filled up.

I placed my hand on hers. 'Pauline, I know how painful this can be for you, but I have to ask. Was Mr. Molloy your father . . . your biological father?'

She sniffled, ran the back of her hand across her eyes, stood, and said, 'I don't know. I don't know anything. I know Craig isn't my real father. That man, Molloy? You say *he* is?'

'How did you know Craig wasn't your natural father?'

'I heard her talk on the phone about it.'

'Heard who?'

'My mother. She doesn't know I know.'

'But you knew nothing about Mr. Molloy?'

'No, I—'

Godfrey ran to us, followed by Jon. 'Ready to head back?' Jon asked.

Pauline and I looked at each other. I tried to convey empathy and sympathy with my eyes, smile, and nod of my head. Whether the message reached her is conjecture. We slowly loaded what was left from the picnic into the suburban and emptied the trash into a wire

211

basket. I was about to enter the vehicle when another car pulled up, driven by homicide investigator Pitura.

'Jim Cook told me you'd come on the raft trip, Mrs. Fletcher. I figured I'd catch you before you went back to the ranch.'

'Your timing is perfect,' I said. 'We were just on our way.'

'How about me driving you back? I'd like to talk to you.'

'All right.'

'See you later,' Jon said, starting the suburban and pulling away. I got in next to Pitura.

'Let's go over to the office,' he said. 'Sheriff Murdie would like to see you.'

'Something official?'

'I don't know. By the way, the Molloys did fly into Gunnison early Sunday evening. Last flight out of Denver. They rented a car at the airport.'

'Interesting.'

'It wouldn't be except for their telling you they'd been driving around seeing the country.'

'Why would they say that?'

'I assumed you'd have that figured out.'

'Sorry to disappoint.'

The Gunnison County Sheriff's office was in a two-story yellow building in Courthouse Square, at the corner of Virginia Avenue and Iowa Street. Sheriff Murdie's office was small and neat, with a single window. I noticed the

212

motto over his desk Pitura had mentioned: 'We will do the impossible at once, miracles take a little longer, magic will be practiced tomorrow.' Murdie was dressed as casually as when we'd first been introduced.

'Good to see you again, Mrs. Fletcher. Please, sit down.'

We passed a few casual comments before he got to the point. 'Mrs. Fletcher, Bob tells me you've been asking plenty of questions out at Powderhorn.'

'I hope I haven't been too obvious. Let's just say I've been doing a lot of socializing.'

Murdie smiled. 'I always appreciate a good euphemism. What sort of answers have you been getting? I mean, during your socializing.'

It was my turn to smile. 'Dribs and drabs.'

'Care to share them with us?'

'I'd like to very much.'

'Good. In a few days the Morrison family will be leaving, which makes it more difficult for us. We'll follow up as much as we need to, but it's always easier, and often more productive, to have suspects nearby.'

'I can imagine.'

\*　　　\*　　　\*

During the next half hour, I was pleased that much of the information I'd managed to gather wasn't a surprise to the sheriff or Bob Pitura. The *Gunnison Country Times* reporter,

Nancy O'Keefe, had shared with them her knowledge of Paul Molloy's past as an alleged arms dealer. I was able to add that the woman in the Denver cabal, Veronica Schwinn, was now Mrs. Craig Morrison.

As we spoke, I remembered Jim Cook saying that according to the deed, the land between his ranch and that owned by the Bureau of Land Management was owned by a Denver group called the V.S. Company. V.S.? Veronica Schwinn? I added that possibility to the mix.

When we'd finished exchanging information, Sheriff Murdie ended the meeting. 'I appreciate your sharing with us what you know, Mrs. Fletcher. I believe in getting information from every possible source. You're helping fill in the picture.'

'But there are still too many pieces missing.'

'We'll find them,' Murdie said. 'In the meantime, a word of advice.'

'Yes?'

'Don't take any risks. There's still a killer at large at the Powderhorn.'

'I'm well aware of that,' I said. 'Don't worry. I may be curious, but I'm not foolhardy.'

'That's good to hear.'

Once outside, Pitura asked if I minded making a stop at the airport on our way back to the ranch.

'Not at all. It's only three o'clock. Ever since taking flying lessons, I'm fascinated with airplanes. I could watch them take off and land all day.'

'Good. Maybe there'll be some air traffic for you to enjoy. I have to meet with someone for twenty minutes, a half hour at the most.'

'Take your time.'

The airport was busy when we arrived, busier than I thought such a small field would be. Pitura mentioned that in ski season it really hops, its extraordinarily long runway accommodating even huge 747s. A Rocky Mountain Air Express flight touched down as we walked from the parking lot into the small, modern terminal. A few private planes, Cessnas and Pipers, came and went.

'I'll be meeting upstairs,' Pitura said. 'Grab yourself a soft drink in the coffee shop. I'll catch up with you there. '

I settled at the counter, ordered an iced tea, and looked out the window at the runway. As I did, the flight crew from the Rocky Mountain Air Express that had just landed—captain, first officer, and flight attendant—came into the shop and took stools next to me. The flight attendant, a pert, shapely, middle-aged woman, looked at me, screwed up her face, and said, 'You're Jessica Fletcher, the mystery writer.'

'That's right,' I said.

'I've read every book you've ever written. I recognized you from all your photos on the book jackets.'

'Nice of you to mention it.'

215

She introduced me to her two male colleagues.

'Where do you get your ideas for stories,' the youthful captain asked.

'Oh, from many sources,' I said.'But frankly, I'm more interested in what *you* do.'

They laughed. 'All we do is take passengers from one place to another,' said the first officer, even younger than the captain. 'Pretty dull.'

'Not to me,' I said. 'I just started taking flying lessons.'

'Really?'

I told them how it came about, and that I was about to make my first solo flight. I didn't mention my other solo flight with Craig Morrison. They were sincerely interested in my decision to learn to fly and asked many questions. I eventually shifted the subject back to them. 'You say it gets dull flying commercially. Why? Too much of a routine?'

'Something like that,' the captain said.

'It's not always dull,' the first officer said, finishing off a piece of apple pie. 'You should have been with us Monday.'

'Why?'

'It was rough,' said the captain, 'the roughest I've ever seen.'

The first officer and flight attendant agreed.

'Everything was flying around the cabin,' the flight attendant said. 'I've flown in heavy weather before, but this was something else.'

'Was it at night?' I asked.

'Afternoon *and* night,' the captain said. 'All crews reported heavy turbulence.'

'That weather missed us,' I said.

'Where were you?'

'The Powderhorn Guest Ranch.'

'Just far enough away,' said the pilot.

They paid, told me to keep up the flying lessons—'Apply for a job with us when you've got your ticket'—and left, passing Bob Pitura as he came in to the coffee shop.

'See, I wasn't too long,' he said.

'I enjoyed myself. Had a conversation with that flight crew.'

'Swapping piloting tales?'

'Something like that. I think I have something else to share with you and the sheriff.'

His eyebrows went up.

'I'll fill you in on the ride back.'


## CHAPTER TWENTY

Because the island next to Cebolla Creek was still sealed off—even if it weren't, it's doubtful any of us would have wanted to gather there around a campfire to toast marshmallows and sing songs—the singalong was relocated to an area on the other side of the lodge. That Jim and Bonnie didn't cancel it was further testimony to their determination to keep things running as normally as possible, murder be dammed.

Every Thursday at the Powderhorn was a Thanksgiving of sorts; the dinner menu was turkey with all the holiday trimmings, capped by a superb creamy pumpkin pie.

'We'll meet for the sing-along and s'mores right after dark,' Bonnie said. 'Wear sweaters. It'll get chilly.'

'I never even want to think about food again,' I said to Seth as we left the lodge and started a walk in the hope of burning off some of the meal.

'I was wondering during dinner why there aren't any fat cowboys.'

'There must be.'

'Ever see one?'

'Now that you challenge me, I must admit I haven't. Being around horses all the time must speed up your metabolism.'

We walked past the stable and down the main road, following Cebolla Creek, accompanied by its bubbling, musical sound. At one point, Seth stopped and did a slow hundred-and-eighty degree turn to ensure we were alone before asking, 'Are you sure it's the way you want to go about this, Jessica?'

'Quite sure. Do you see any problems with it?'

'Always the possibility of a problem where murderers are concerned.'

'I mean, do you see any gaps in my reasoning?'

He laughed softly. 'That's always a loaded question, coming from you, Jessica.'

'I'll take that to mean you don't see any . . . gaps.'

'What I think isn't as important as what the sheriff and his sidekick, Pitura, think. You went over the entire plan with them?'

'Yes. When I told Bob Pitura what I'd learned at the airport, he insisted we turn around and go back to Sheriff Murdie's office. I discussed every aspect of it with them. They think it might work.'

'And you talked to that reporter, O'Keefe?'

'Right. When I was finished with the sheriff and Pitura, I caught up with her at the paper. Her final bits of intelligence made me realize how right I am.'

'Should be quite an evening.'

'If it goes the way I plan.'

'Had a chance to run it by Jim and Bonnie yet?'

'I talked briefly with Jim. We agreed to get together after the sing-along, at their house.'

'Am I invited?'

'You're the guest of honor, Seth.'

\*     \*     \*

Despite the change of venue, the gathering around the campfire was pleasant and entertaining. Most of the Morrison clan was there, the two teenagers and Cousin William the absentees. One of the wranglers, Andy Wilson, a lovely young man from Texas, sang and played the guitar. He had a plaintive voice filled with emotion, especially when he sang a song written by the country singer Ricky Skaggs, 'Thanks Again,' which Andy sang as a tribute to his own parents of whom he'd often spoken during the week.

Seth and I returned to my cabin following the sing-along and waited until Jim and Bonnie had cleaned up the area and returned to their house. We checked that no one was outside my cabin before leaving, and joined them in their living room.

'Now,' Jim said, 'let's go over what you told me this afternoon.'

'Okay. Your local reporter, Nancy O'Keefe, has a close friend in Washington, D.C. He's a journalist, with a ton of close connections within the government, particularly the intelligence community. He fed Ms. O'Keefe the background on Paul Molloy.'

'The arms dealing?' Bonnie said.

'Right. When Ms. O'Keefe mentioned that some intelligence agency had learned of negotiations between Molloy and Libya concerning the sale of weapons-grade uranium, I thought back to our Jeep ride. Molloy wanted that land you showed me. By the way, the owner, the V.S. Company, is actually the Morrison family. Veronica Morrison's maiden name was Schwinn. She's the 'VS' in the V.S. Company.'

'Are you saying that Mr. Molloy was murdered over that land?' Bonnie asked.

'I believe so,' I said.

'What about Mrs. Molloy?' Jim asked.

'I don't know,' I said. 'Maybe our little show Saturday night will answer that question.'

'What about that picture of the youngster, Pauline?' Jim asked. 'If she is Molloy's daughter, wouldn't that be a stronger motive for murder than a business conflict over a piece of land?'

'It could be, but I don't think it was the reason for Molloy's murder. The question is, can we do tomorrow what I've suggested?'

Jim and Bonnie looked at each other.

'I think so,' Jim said.

'It'll have to be away from the ranch,' Seth said. 'We can't arouse anyone's suspicion.'

'That won't be a problem,' Jim said. 'The Morrisons are taking an all-day ride up into the hills. They'll be gone from nine till four.'

'The staff can't know, either,' I said.

'How about the Powderhorn Community Center?' Bonnie suggested.

'I pointed it out to you on Sunday coming in from the airport,' Jim said.

'I remember it,' I said. 'It won't be used tomorrow?'

'Seldom is,' Bonnie said. 'Mostly evening

functions. It should be yours for the day.'

'Perfect. Can we go there right after the group leaves on the ride?'

'Sure.

'And you'll have the video you've been shooting with you?'

'Yup.'

Seth and I walked back to our cabins.

'I'm not sure I'll be able to sleep,' I said.

'A little too much adventure, Jessica?'

I laughed. 'It's more than I bargained for when we came here,' I said. 'Two murders. You falling off a horse. International arms dealers. An illegitimate daughter. A hair-raising plane ride. Yes, enough adventure to last a long time.'

'And more to come. Good night, Jessica. No matter what happens, you know I'm with you.'

'Just as you've always been.' I kissed his cheek, and we hugged. And I wiped a tear from my eye as I walked away.


## CHAPTER TWENTY-ONE

Jim Cook, Seth, a video technician from the Gunnison Sheriff's Department, and I spent almost all day Friday at the Community Center, Powderhorn's former one-room schoolhouse that was closed when the kids started being bussed to Gunnison, then sold to the town by the school board. It had a small stage with a curtain like a large window shade, on which Gunnison businesses bought advertising space. I felt guilty keeping Jim from his duties at the ranch, but every time I mentioned it, he replied with his usual engaging laugh, 'Bonnie will handle it, Jess. She does everything anyway. I'm just the handsome, suave figurehead.'

The video tech returned to Gunnison, and we arrived back at the ranch minutes before the Morrisons rode in from their all-day outing on horseback. At dinner—it was pizza night, the best I've ever eaten—Jim detailed the next day's activities. There would be the morning ride at nine, then a gymkhana at two in the afternoon in which guests would compete on horseback for prizes to be awarded Saturday night, along with awards for the biggest fish caught, and a showing of the week's videotape.

'I see the police are no longer here,' Evelyn said.

Chris Morrison's laugh was derisive. 'Those clowns have probably given up. They ought to stick to getting cats out of trees and finding lost dogs.'

'To the contrary,' Jim said. 'I heard this afternoon that they've narrowed in on the killer.'

All eyebrows went up.

'Who is he?' Veronica asked.

'A drifter who settled in here a few months

back. He's been camping out in the shack Uncle Irvy used to live in.'

'Who's Uncle Irvy?' Robert Morrison asked.

'A hermit, a strange loner but a decent man. His shack is back in the hills near one of the abandoned mines. Lived off the land, always filthy—'

'But sweet,' Bonnie added.

'What about this drifter?' Craig asked. 'What's his name?'

'Not sure,' Jim said. 'They say he's a distant relation of Alfred Packer.'

'The cannibal?' Robert Morrison asked.

'One and the same,' Jim said. 'Packer killed and ate five men to get through a severe winter back in the late eighteen-seventies. He was convicted in Lake City, but never hanged. The judge told him at the sentencing, 'You man-eating SOB, there were only seven Democrats in Hinsdale County and you had to go and eat five of 'em.' They eventually let him out of prison when he was dying of some disease. Governor Lamb pardoned him posthumously about ten years ago because he said Packer did more for Colorado tourism than any other person in the state's history.'

'That's disgusting,' Evelyn said.

'But true,' Jim said. 'Every word of it.'

'Back to this drifter,' Robert Morrison said. 'They've arrested him?'

'I believe so,' Bonnie said. 'Have some dessert. We call it Impossible Cherry Pie.'

*　　*　　*

I realized I'd been on horseback only twice since arriving at the ranch, and wanted to enjoy it one last time, so I went on the Saturday morning ride. Bonnie also convinced me to take part in the afternoon gymkhana. Seth, understandably, declined any suggestions that he saddle up again. 'I'll be happy to watch and applaud,' he said.

Pauline Morrison was on the morning ride, along with her grandmother, mother, and father. Pauline and I didn't speak to each other until we were on the way back and Crystal Kildare, our wrangler, and the Morrison adults had gotten ahead of us, leaving Pauline and me out of their earshot.

'I hope I didn't upset you on Thursday,' I said.

'It's okay.'

'I have the feeling you did know that Mr. Molloy was your natural father, Pauline.'

'Why?'

'Because of how upset you were when he was killed,'

She said nothing.

'Pauline, I found your diary at Hidden Lake.'

Her pretty, freckled young face flared into anger.

'You have every right to hate me for looking

at it, Pauline, but two people have been brutally killed. Mr. Molloy *was* your biological father.'

'Pauline, come here!' Evelyn shouted from where she'd stopped on the trail.

Pauline continued to glare at me, eyes narrowed, lips trembling.

Evelyn turned her horse and started back.

'I do hate you,' Pauline said, digging her heels into her horse's side and riding to meet her grandmother.

Poor girl, I thought. The family in which she was growing up might be wealthy, but it was morally bankrupt. That didn't excuse me for having violated her inner thoughts by reading those few pages that comprised her diary. But there are times, I think, when the end does justify the means, in this case to help solve the barbarous murder of a man and a woman. Whether it was wrong of me to intrude upon her private life was something I'd have to grapple with in the days to come. One thing was certain from having read the diary. She not only knew that Craig wasn't her natural father, she knew it was Paul Molloy.

After a lunch of chili and toasted cheese sandwiches, we headed for the corral and the gymkhana. I didn't ride well, but the wranglers enthusiastically applauded my efforts, as did Seth. Although the results wouldn't be announced until that night, we all knew that Evelyn Morrison would probably win, along

226

with her older son, Craig. Both were skilled riders.

The dinner steak fry was scheduled to be held on the island, but like the sing-along, was moved to where we'd sat around the bonfire on Thursday night. I'd arranged for Seth and me to host a predinner cocktail party. Bonnie added liquor to the daily shopping list, and Joel and Sue helped us set up. To our surprise, all the adult Morrisons showed up, and they were in good spirits.

'This is a lovely thing you're doing,' Robert, Evelyn's attorney brother, told me. He actually smiled.

'Our pleasure,' I said. 'Always nice to get together for a drink with good people, especially when the cloud of being murder suspects isn't hanging over our heads any longer.'

'You were never a suspect,' he said.

'Not true,' I said. 'The sheriff and his people were looking at me and Seth with as much scrutiny as they looked at anyone else. We're just relieved it's over.'

Craig Morrison joined us. 'Glad you didn't stay mad about the flight,' he said, flashing his crooked, thick-lipped smile.

'Don't be silly,' I said. 'You did me a service. I flew without anyone telling me how to do it and landed safely on a grass strip. I'm rarin' to go on my solo the minute we get home.'

'Good for you.'

As the Morrisons drifted away, Seth whispered in my ear, 'Looks like everyone's considerably more relaxed this evening.'

'Seems that way.'

'Nice party.'

'Very nice. It's good to see everyone in a good mood after such a difficult week.'

'Hearing that the police have identified the killer as not being from our cozy little group seems to have done wonders for the spirits.'

I smiled. 'As we knew it would. Excuse me. I should mingle with our guests.'

*     *     *

After dinner of steaks cooked to perfection, we gathered in the lodge's main room for coffee and the evening's activities. Jim served as the MC. First on the program was the awarding of prizes. There were no surprises. Evelyn took top honors in the gymkhana, with her son, Craig, coming in second. Seth received an honorary award for 'the week's best fall from a horse.' The two teenagers received token riding prizes, and Godfrey had caught the biggest fish. It wasn't very big at all, but there had been little fishing that week, to my chagrin. I just knew that trout I'd hooked, and lost, was still there waiting for me.

'Well, is everyone ready for their screen debut?' Jim asked.

We indicated we were.

'Oh, before we get to that,' he said, 'I have to tell you a story. Bob Morrison, as most of you know, had a toothache this week. Fortunately, it seems to have healed itself. But I'd called our dentist in Gunnison just in case he was needed. He told me he had a patient come in just that morning with a serious problem.

'Seems our dentist had made a full upper plate for this patient about six months ago, but the plate was all rotted out. The dentist said he'd never seen anything like it. He asked the patient whether he'd been eating anything unusual.

'The patient told him his wife is always making asparagus with hollandaise sauce.'

'That's it!' the dentist said. 'It's all that lemon juice in the hollandaise that rotted your upper plate. I'll make you a new one made out of chrome.'

'Chrome?' the patient said. 'That'll look funny.'

'Do you know what the dentist told the patient?'

'What did the dentist tell the patient, Jim?' Seth and I asked in concert.

He sang his response to the tune of the popular Christmas song: 'There's no plate like chrome for the hollandaise.'

Mixed groans and laughter from the guests.

'Okay,' Jim said. 'Time for the video of the week's activities. Fortunately, I didn't have my camera to document the two unplanned activities—' He paused for effect. 'Murder!'

There was some uncomfortable shifting of chairs.

'All right,' he said, 'Lights! Action! Camera!'

Bonnie turned off the lights, and the large TV screen came to life.

It started with the arrival of guests on Sunday. Seth and I were seen leaving Jim and Bonnie's house after tea, Socks and Holly racing around our feet, and Jim took additional footage of us on the porch of my cabin. The next group to arrive were the Morrisons, in their limousines from Gunnison, all except Craig, who would fly in later Sunday afternoon.

There was footage of us at dinner Sunday night. Jim panned our faces, pausing at each, hoping for a reaction. Young Godfrey obliged by sticking out his tongue.

The Molloys' late arrival was captured, although Jim was busy and grabbed only a few seconds of them at the table. There were a few postprandial shots of us milling about the lodge, and the staff lined up for a group picture.

The second segment of the video showed breakfast Monday morning. Then it was out to the corral, where Crystal's riding lessons were captured. The two groups, the novices and the more experienced, were seen riding from the corral in the direction of the road.

The staff dominated the next sequence, Jim building a montage of them handling their chores, most of them involving the horses and their care. Chief wrangler Joe Walker was seen treating with tender loving care one of the herd suffering from strangles. Jim must have handed the camera to someone else because his face suddenly filled the screen, and he said, 'Joe here knows more about treating horses than any vet I've ever met.'

There were a few random shots of the ranch, some of which included glimpses of the police presence following the discovery of Paul Molloy's body. Veronica Morrison's arrival now dominated the screen. She was seen exiting the large suburban vehicle driven by wrangler Jon Adler. It was a wide shot to begin with. But as Socks and Holly joined the Cooks in the greeting, encircling her, Jim zoomed in tight on her feet.

That shot suddenly froze on the screen. Chris Morrison laughed. 'Nice shoes, Veronica.' The longer the still-frame remained, the more comments came from those in the room. Had the camera malfunctioned? some wondered. Was this another Jim Cook joke, video-style?

Those questions were answered when my face replaced the picture of Veronica's shoes. 'As you know,' my recorded voice said, 'I'm Jessica Fletcher, a guest this week at the Powderhorn, just as you are.'

'What's going on?' Robert Morrison asked.

I answered from the screen as the shot of Veronica's shoes reappeared. 'Please notice that her shoes have mud caked on them, and that there are two burrs stuck to the bottom of her slacks.'

More laughter now. The consensus in the room was that this was a joke.

'Mrs. Morrison said she arrived by plane Monday afternoon. It rained late Sunday night. Judging from the mud on those shoes, Mrs. Morrison must have been walking at some point on muddy ground.'

The laughter turned to instant silence.

'On with the show,' I said.

A flurry of comments and questions were interrupted as the video started running again, depicting routine ranch activities. As it ran, I quietly got up from where I was sitting and retreated to the dining room, from where I could still see the screen and the people watching it. Joel Louden and Sue Wennington were almost finished cleaning up the dining room and kitchen, stopping frequently in their chores to see what was going on in the darkened other room.

'What was that all about?' Louden asked me.

'What?'

'You on the video talking about her shoes.'

I laughed lightly. 'Oh, just having fun. Stay tuned. There's more to come.'

The guests settled down as the video continued to show ranch scenes—the guests captured going about their daily activities; taking riding lessons; Godfrey and his uncle, Chris, fishing; swimming in the pool; lolling in the hot tub next to the pool; gathered for meals in the dining room; all those things that guests of the Powderhorn Guest Ranch have been enjoying for years.

But then the scene on the screen faded into another one distinctly not of ranch life. Reporter Nancy O'Keefe was seated in her office at the newspaper. What the audience couldn't see was the video technician from the sheriff's office taping her from behind the camera. He'd done it the night before we went to work at the Powderhorn Community Center.

'I'm Nancy O'Keefe, a reporter for the *Gunnison Country Times*. Gunnison may be a small town, and this newspaper a small town paper, but that doesn't mean we don't chase big stories.'

This interruption in the ranch video—the Morrisons were well aware of the departure from the standard Saturday night video because they'd sat through it when they'd been guests before—caused another round of questions.

'There have been two murders at the Powderhorn,' Nancy continued. 'A Paul Molloy and his alleged wife, Geraldine. But of course, you already know that. What you don't know is *who* they really were, and I'm here to tell you.'

'Hey, what the hell is going on here?' Craig Morrison asked loudly, looking for Jim Cook in the darkness.

Veronica, who sat between her husband and her mother-in-law, Evelyn, turned and looked back to where I stood. I had the feeling she was about to get up and leave.

Nancy O'Keefe continued. 'Paul Molloy was once reputed to be an international arms dealer, peddling weapons to rogue countries at odds with the United States. They never convicted him of anything, or at least that was the official line. In reality, they cut a deal with him. By "them" I mean the government. They let him off the hook in return for helping them, the government, identify others in the same dirty business. That's why he came to the Powderhorn Ranch, to help in an investigation.'

Veronica stood. So did Jim Cook. 'Why don't you stay through to the end,' he said to her.

'What's the point of this,' Robert Morrison asked.

Jim, put his index finger to his lips. 'Shhhhhh,' he said. 'Let's hear what she has to say.'

'The woman who said she was Paul Molloy's wife, Geraldine, was a government agent,' O'Keefe continued. 'She'd been working undercover on this case for the U.S. Customs Department.'

Veronica started to leave, but her husband grabbed her arm. 'Relax, sweetie. You can't walk out on a good movie. You'll miss the ending.'

I replaced Nancy O'Keefe on the screen. 'I've been taking flying lessons. If I hadn't, I probably wouldn't have spent time at the Gunnison Airport on Thursday. Interesting what you can learn talking to pilots. They said the flying weather on Monday afternoon was terrible, the worst they'd ever seen. You, Mrs. Morrison—may I call you Veronica?—you said you'd flown in to Gunnison on Monday, but you also said the flight was 'smooth as silk.' I think you arrived on Sunday. The weather on Sunday was smooth—as silk.'

Scenes from Seth's fall from his horse, and his rescue up the steep incline, now flooded the screen.

Bonnie raised the lights slightly, allowing people to see each other, as well as the video.

Veronica stood again, shook off her husband's grasp, and made her way to where I stood with Joel Louden, the cook. She gave me a hard look. then turned to see who would follow her. No one did. Although the video continued to run, all eyes were now on us.

'Veronica,' I said, now speaking directly, 'there's no sense leaving. The sheriff and his people are outside waiting for you.'

'You don't know what you're talking about,' she said.

'I think you know that what I'm saying is correct—Ms. Schwinn.'

My use of her maiden name startled her. The defiant look was replaced by a flash of panic. It lasted only a second.

'When did you and Mr. Molloy have your affair?' I asked.

'What are you talking about?'

'This.' I handed her the photo of Pauline that had been in Molloy's wallet. She looked at it, made a disgusted face, and dropped the photo to the floor.

'You go back a long way, don't you?' I said, referring to her and Paul Molloy.

'That's none of your business.'

'Correct, except your long-standing relationship resulted in his murder—*and* the murder of a government undercover agent.'

I don't know what tended to unravel her more, what I was saying, or the fact no one came from the main room to stand by her.

'Why did you kill him?' I asked.

'I didn't kill anyone.'

'Are we being literal?'

'What do you mean by that?'

'You might not have rammed the rasp into his chest, or bludgeoned Geraldine—by the way, her real name was Geraldine Jankowksi—but you ordered it done.'

'I've had enough. Excuse me, Mrs. Fletcher,

you're in my way and I don't like it.'

As she slowly, nonchalantly walked to the door, I turned to Joel Louden. 'Going with her?' I asked.

Veronica's departure brought others from the main room. The rest of the Morrison adults stood close together, their faces void of expression.

I smiled at them. 'You all knew what she was up to, didn't you?'

'You've got your killer,' Evelyn said. 'Now I suggest we all go to our cabins and enjoy what's left of the evening.'

I again looked at Louden. 'Well?' I asked.

He looked from person to person, then directly at me.

'She's waiting for you, Joel. You should have stuck to a hot kitchen. The heat put on a murderer is more than anyone can bear.'

Louden bolted from us, flung open the door, and rushed outside where Sheriff Murdie, Investigator Pitura, and four uniformed officers stood in a group. We followed. Veronica Morrison could be seen walking toward the road. Louden ran after her.

'They're heading for the air strip,' I said.

'Aren't you going to go after them?' Jim Cook asked Sheriff Murdie.

'No need,' I said. 'They aren't flying anywhere tonight.' I held up the key for the Cessna parked at the grass strip. I'd taken it earlier in the day from beneath the left-hand seat.

'Round them up at the strip,' Murdie told his uniformed men.

Pitura said to the Morrisons, 'I think we should go back inside and do some talking. I'm sure there are a few questions Mrs. Fletcher and I would like answered.'

We filed back into the lodge. The only person who hadn't come outside was Pauline Morrison. She was crouched on the floor, her discarded childhood picture in her hands. I bent over, placed my hand on her shoulder, and said, 'I'm sorry.'

She responded by crushing the picture in her hand and running out into the night.

## CHAPTER TWENTY-TWO

Veronica Morrison and Joel Louden were taken away by Gunnison police to be charged with the murder of Paul Molloy and Geraldine Jankowski. The rest of the Morrison family asked to have limousines dispatched immediately to the ranch to drive them to Gunnison, where they'd ordered a private jet to pick them up.

'I assure you, Mr. and Mrs. Cook, that you will never see us again at this ranch,' Robert Morrison said.

'Sorry to hear that,' Jim said, glancing at Bonnie and stifling a smile. She, too, was successful at masking her giddiness.

While the Morrisons packed, Seth and I sat with Jim and Bonnie in their living room, a large picture window affording a view of the ranch.

'Bob Pitura says he doesn't think charges can be brought against the rest of the family, at least not for these murders,' Jim said, 'but he's passing along whatever he has to federal authorities. If what you say is true, Jess, this family business is more than land development.'

'I suspect that's the case,' I said. 'The only reason Mr. Molloy and Ms. Jankowski could have had for being here was to investigate the Morrisons' plans for the land adjacent to your ranch.'

'What upsets me is that we hired the actual killer.' Bonnie wrapped her arms about herself and shuddered. 'We never should have taken Joel on without checking his background.'

'You were in a bind,' Seth offered. 'Happens to everyone.'

'He certainly wasn't reluctant to talk,' Jim said. 'Started babbling the minute they put the cuffs on him down at the landing strip. Ms. Veronica Morrison was quite the swinger, having an affair all those years ago with Molloy when they were secret partners in arms dealing, and sleeping with Joel. No wonder her

239

husband didn't offer a word on her behalf. Probably happy to see her spend the rest of her life in jail.'

'The grandmother, too,' Seth said. 'No love lost there.'

'Joel said Veronica convinced him to put that other rasp on the grass to focus suspicion on the wranglers,' Jim said.

'And he claims it was Veronica who shoved it into Molloy, although I doubt that,' Seth said. 'He admits they confronted Molloy together. Seems more likely that he did the deadly deed, with her cheering him on.'

'How did you narrow in on him, Jess?' Bonnie asked.

'No one thing, Bonnie, just an amalgamation of factors. He lied about having been the last person to see her alive when he brought dinner to the honeymoon cabin. Sue was supposed to do it, but Joel switched the schedule at the last minute. Also, he took off Sunday night to—I think you said—see a friend in Gunnison. That gave him the opportunity to pick up Veronica, drive her back here for her clandestine meeting with Molloy, kill him, then drive her back to town. The fact that he just seemed to show up here when you needed a substitute cook and was from Las Vegas, where Molloy had been living, added to the mix. I suggested to Bob Pitura that he check Gunnison motels. Sure enough, the night clerk at one of them identified Joel from a photo I took off the bulletin board in front of the lodge. It was convenient having all those Polaroid shots of staff. The clerk said Joel checked in late Sunday night with a stunning blond woman, but left a half hour after arriving. I'm sure that same clerk will identify Veronica, too, when he's shown a picture of her.'

'By the way, Jessica, did you ever figure out who was spying on you down by the creek?'

'No, but it doesn't matter. No harm came from it. I have a feeling it was William, Cousin Willy. A sad soul. I read his science fiction story. It was, to be kind, not very good.'

'We owe a debt to Nancy O'Keefe,' Bonnie said.

'We certainly do,' I said. 'Without her, none of Molloy's background would be known to us.'

'I'll give her a call and see if she'd like to have brunch tomorrow. Plenty of food now that we're the only ones here, along with the staff. I'll see if Bob and April Pitura and Sheriff Murdie and his wife can make it, too.'

'Looks like I'm back in the kitchen,' Bonnie said.

'And a good thing,' Jim said. 'Bonnie's as good a cook as anybody we hire.'

'Poor Pauline,' I said. 'Not only is she the daughter of someone other than the man supposed to be her father, her mother is about

241

to be charged with double murder.'

'Breaks your heart,' Bonnie said.

'I just hope she has the strength to overcome it,' I said.

The limos arrived, and the Morrisons got in them without another word to anyone. We stood in front of the house and watched them drive away. Jim waved. Bonnie was no longer able to keep her pleasure under wraps, and sighed with relief. We all did.

'Glad to be rid of them,' Jim said. 'All season long we have the nicest people in the world coming here, good and decent folks who enjoy themselves. After a week, it becomes one big family. Lots of them stay close long after they're gone.'

Socks ran up and offered me a stick.

'No, you don't,' I said.

'I think he deserves a little play,' Seth said, pulling the stick from the dog's mouth and throwing it.

'You're breaking the rules,' I said.

'Seems you've been breaking them ever since we got here, Jessica.'

\*     \*     \*

Sheriff Murdie couldn't accept Jim's invitation for Sunday morning brunch, but the Pituras did, along with Nancy O'Keefe.

'Sorry to see you folks leave,' Pitura said. 'Enjoy your stay?'

'It was . . . an adventure,' I answered.

'You and Seth had better make plans to get back here, and soon,' Jim said. 'I promise you there won't be any more murders.'

'Happy to take you up on your offer,' Seth said, helping himself to another stack of pancakes. 'Anxious to get back on a horse.'

'Even after what happened to you?' Bonnie asked.

'Nothing like a little adventure in one's life. Am I right, Jessica?'

'Yes, Seth, you are right,'

'I always knew it was Joel,' Sue Wennington said as she cleared my plate. 'He was a weirdo.'

'Turned out that way,' I said.

'You know, Bonnie, I'm a real good cook,' Sue said. 'Happy to take Joel's place for the rest of the season.'

'I think I'll take you up on it,' Bonnie said. 'Isn't it time we headed for the airport?'

'Certainly is,' Jim said.

'We'll take you into town,' April Pitura said.

'Thanks, but we want to spend every possible minute with our friends from Maine,' Bonnie said. 'It's been too long.'

'We'll be anxious to hear how things turn out,' I said.

'I'll keep Jim and Bonnie informed,' Pitura said.

We arrived at the airport in plenty of time

Boston plane. We kissed, hugged, and shed some tears.

'Remember now,' said Bonnie, 'you promised to come back within the year.'

'Count on it,' I said. 'I might even fly us here once I have my pilot's license.'

Seth coughed.

'Before you go,' Jim said, 'I don't think I told you about my experience with a snake when I was driving guests in the Jeep a while back.'

'A snake?' I asked.

'Yup. Biggest snake I ever saw. Stopped just before I ran him over. His name was Nate.'

'A snake named Nate,' Seth said. 'I sense one of your stories coming on.' Jim laughed and continued. 'I got talking to this snake and asked him what he was doing in the middle of the road. He pointed to a big bush with his tail end and told me it was his responsibility to keep anyone from pulling a lever in the middle of that bush. He said that if anyone pulled the lever, the world would blow up. By now, the guests in the Jeep thought I was crazy talking to a snake, so I got back behind the wheel and took off.

'I was back on that road alone the next day and there was Nate. Problem was I didn't see him until it was too late. Ran him over and killed him. You know the moral of this story?'

'No, Jim, what's the moral of this story?'

'Better Nate than lever.'

*       *       *

Seth and I and four others from Cabot Cove returned to the Powderhorn Guest Ranch ten months later, two weeks after Veronica Morrison and Joel Louden had been convicted and sentenced in a Denver courtroom for the murders of Paul Molloy and Geraldine Jankowski. A month prior to that, major newspapers reported that two companies, Morrison, Ltd. and the V.S. Company, had been indicted for illegal arms sales to Libya. Part of the story focused on their plans to mine uranium on the tract of land between Jim and Bonnie's ranch and BLM land under the guise of mining for gold and silver. Briefly mentioned was a former partner in the V.S. Company's scheme, Paul Molloy, now deceased.

'Did you ever get your pilot's license?' Jim asked on our first night at the ranch.

I proudly handed him my license to fly single-engine, land aircraft.

'Congratulations,' Bonnie said, then turned to Seth. 'Have you been up with her yet?'

'Haven't found the time,' he replied.

I smiled sweetly at him. At least he didn't express what he'd admitted to me, that he would be uncomfortable going up in a plane with me as the pilot.

245

'Always a first time,' Jim said. 'How about renting a plane in Gunnison and taking us all for a ride?'

'When in Powderhorn, do as the Powderhornians do,' I said, not sure whether that's what residents of Powderhorn were called. 'Horses, not planes. Maybe on our next trip here.'

The second visit was everything the first one wasn't—no murders, no nasty people—just pleasant rides into the Colorado mountains, delicious food, sing-alongs around a roaring campfire, days and nights spent with wonderful people, and for me a good deal of fishing. I caught a trout my first day on Cebolla Creek and was certain it was the one that got away almost a year before. I gently released him and promised I'd be back again.

A promise I intend to keep.

We hope you have enjoyed this Large Print book. Other Chivers Press or G.K. Hall & Co. Large Print books are available at your library or directly from the publishers.

For more information about current and forthcoming titles, please call or write, without obligation, to:

Chivers Press Limited
Windsor Bridge Road
Bath BA2 3AX
England
Tel. (01225) 335336

OR

G.K. Hall & Co.
P.O. Box 159
Thorndike, Maine 04986
USA
Tel. (800) 223-2336

All our Large Print titles are designed for easy reading, and all our books are made to last.